JABBERWOCK

JABBERWOCK

JABBERWOCK

Nowhere USA Book One

NINIE HAMMON

STERLING & STONE

Chapter One

"Hurted me," was all Merrie said, swiping ineffectually at the gush of blood pouring down her forehead, over her eyebrow and into her left eye.

Charlie McClintock turned from the books she was stacking in a packing box, expecting a skinned knee requiring a kiss to make it better. When she saw the blood, she couldn't help burping out a tiny scream, which, of course, let three-year-old Merrie know that the cut on her forehead was, after all, something worthy of pitching a fit over. And so she did.

Dropping dramatically to her knees, Merrie tilted her head back and began to wail, a high-pitched screech that should have etched the sound syllables into the glass in the windows. Charlie took two steps and scooped the little girl up into her arms, mumbling soothing words — "Shhh, sokay, shhhh, momma's gotcha, shhhhh" — trying to keep the child still long enough to examine the wound.

Ordinarily, Charlene Reneé McClintock was not a woman easily rattled, but she hadn't been able to go back to sleep after last night's freak storm and the violent fury of it left her ... unsettled. It had struck without warning, no rumble of thunder to signal its approach. It hadn't even been sprinkling when a sudden wind savagely attacked the house, tearing the front screen door off its hinges and ripping the porch swing off its chains to use as a battering ram against the wall. A strobe of lightning burned into Charlie's retina the image of the front-yard willow tree's branches lashing out like a cat o' nine tails, the juniper trees cavorting like those blow-up figures you see at car dealerships and grand openings, ripped-off limbs threatening to come crashing through the windows ... and then it was over.

It didn't ratchet down in ferocity. It just ... *stopped.* Blew through and was gone in — what? Three minutes? Five? When she'd stepped out on the porch to survey the damage, she could see stars twinkling in the velvet black sky.

A twister perhaps? How could you have a tornado without an accompanying thunderstorm? There hadn't been a drop of rain. And the fresh, after-a-storm smell in the air ... it wasn't there. She smelled only the honeysuckle around the porch. She'd been in a hurricane once in South Florida and it had been no more ferocious. That'd make the record books: The Appalachian Hurricane of June 1995.

It wasn't just the ferocity of the storm, though. It was the sound it'd made. The wind had ... wailed. Sounded like crying children ... or lost souls in hell. Now, maybe that was the normal sound of a hurricane in the mountains — hard to know a thing like that when there was no such thing as a mountain hurricane. But perhaps last night's storm was holding up for Charlie McClintock's inspection the outside edges of "no such thing."

Who knew?

Well, what she did know was that the cut on Meredith's forehead, far from as life-threatening as the amount of blood would seem to indicate, did need a couple of stitches. And unless Charlie wanted the little girl to carry for the rest of her life a permanent reminder on her forehead of tripping over a storm-tossed tree branch in her grandmother's driveway, the sewing should be done by a plastic surgeon. That certainly wasn't going to happen if she took Merrie to the emergency room at the Beaufort County Hospital in Carlisle.

But where else could she go?

She couldn't haul a screaming three-year-old all the way to Lexington! And Nower County, Kentucky had no hospital.

Nower County, Kentucky had no … *anything*.

Charlie was facing a half hour's drive through the mountains with a bleeding, shrieking toddler strapped into a car seat behind her.

Goody.

Chapter Two

Viola Tackett's teeth clacked together when the old pickup truck slammed down into a hole big as a soup pot in the logging road and she made herself a promise: I ain't doing this no more.

She hadn't ought to be doing it now, but until she was lead-pipe certain that Neb, Obie, and Zach knew what they was doing, she didn't dare leave it to them without her coming along behind to check. Shoot, them boys was forty years old. You'd think they could handle a little thing like planting marijuana seedlings with a tobacco setter. But wasn't none of the three smart enough to pour sand out of a boot if the instructions was on the heel, so here she was bouncing around in the old truck on the way for a surprise inspection.

She come around a bend and slammed on the brakes — had to push the pedal all the way to the floor because them brake pads was flat as week-old roadkill. Barely got stopped before she ran right into the tree lying across the road, so big it must have been a sapling when Abraham

4

Lincoln was a pup over in LaRue County a century and a half ago. Okay, maybe that was a stretch, but she couldn't imagine how it had stood as long as it had, big as it was. The fierce winds of last night's storm must have took it out.

It'd been a storm unlike any Viola'd seen in near seventy years drawing breath at the good Lord's pleasure on this earth where he put her. The wind was the thing. She had a log cabin sat snug as a dung beetle in a cow patty, had been built by her granddaddy back before the First World War. She'd been born there, would likely die there and had birthed her children, the five that'd lived and the three that hadn't — all except the twins she sent back to the devil — in the same bed where they'd been conceived.

But even snug as it was, the wind last night was peculiar. Wasn't like no ordinary wind, and she told Neb, who'd got drunk and missed the whole thing, that it sounded like it was … crying, had a sound like a baby wailing off in the trees, like to broke Viola's heart.

And wasn't much in life broke Viola Tackett's heart.

She had to throw her shoulder against the pickup truck door twice 'fore it'd open. Latch was broke and she supposed not being able to open the door was a sight better than not being able to close it. She walked around to the front of the truck to have a look-see at the downed tree but it was a waste of time. Wasn't no way she'd ever be able to move it, not even if she tied a chain to it and pulled it with the truck. She'd send the boys out here with chainsaws to clear the road soon's they got back to the house. But that was then and this was now. She sighed.

Wasn't nothin' for it but to take the branch road that went up over Bent Stick Ridge. It was ten miles out of the way if it was a foot, wound all the way into Drayton

County and back into Nower County, but wasn't nothing else she could do 'less she wanted to turn her flat butt around and haul it back to the house and that wasn't gonna happen.

Viola climbed back up into her truck and eased the old thing into reverse. You had to hold your mouth just right to get it into and out of gears. Transmission was shot. But the old truck was like an old dog and she wasn't ready yet to put it down, even if it was held together with Bondo and duct tape.

Heading back down the mountain, retracing her steps up it, to the fork where the other logging road took out east gave her time to think, and 'course her mind went to what she'd ought to do about Malachi. Wasn't nothing but a rooster chasing its own tail feathers to consider it because wasn't nothing she *could* do about Malachi. The boy was hurting, bleeding inside where you couldn't see it, and she was watching him sink further and further into himself every day.

Malachi was her baby. Well, no, Esther Ruth was her baby, always would be. She wouldn't never be more than six or seven years old and even though she was a woman full growed, she still lit up like a Fourth-of-July sparkler whenever she seen Viola and cried out "Mommy!" before racing to give her a hug. Esther would stay a child forever.

But Malachi was the youngest, the only one of the lot of them had a lick of sense. He was the one of her boys that she'd always intended to run things for her, the one who'd take over the "thriving family business" she'd spent her whole life trying to build. Her enterprises had ebbed and flowed with the commerce of the world outside the mountains over the years, but didn't none of them *thrive*.

'Course there'd always been shine. She'd took that over

from her daddy — what was left of him when she got done with him. She'd run a chop shop at one time out of a garage down on Rabbit Run Road. Cars stolen off the streets of Lexington was reduced to unidentifiable car parts in less than an afternoon, drove in one side and come out the other in pieces. She'd fenced other stolen goods, too, had run a couple of rings of prostitutes that worked the coal fields, collected protection money every week from mom-and-pop businesses as far away as the West Virginia line.

There'd been money to be made growing weed back 'fore everybody got their panties in a wad about it when they busted the Cornbread Mafia over in Marion County six years ago. Anymore, it was almost more hassle than it was worth, had to hide it between plants in a cornfield, grow a little patch here, a little there.

In the last few years, they'd been what the big-city newspapers called an "epidemic of addiction" in the mountains — to a little white pill called OxyContin. Of course, she elbowed her way to the front of the line to make a buck on the drug, but it was hard to turn a profit on something you couldn't manufacture yourself, when you was at the mercy of some sleazy drug dealer who charged whatever he thought he could squeeze out of you.

For a right smart while now Viola'd been struggling to control a growing rage that life wasn't never gonna give her what she'd spent all her years chasing. Springtime come and went and come again, and with each new turning of the seasons the anger in her belly grew. It was one thing to have a yearning inside, chewing at your guts like a lazy rat when you was *young*, looking at years stacked up on top of each other out *in front* of you. It was another thing alto-gether to have the pile of years *behind* you, watching the time grow short and your dream still hanging there out of reach.

Far as the world knew, Viola Tackett was a workhorse who intended to die in the harness, a woman who'd still be out there scrambling while they was shoveling in the dirt.

She scoffed at "retirement." Said she'd read the Bible through cover to cover so many times she'd about wore the print off the pages, and she hadn't never run across the part that said you could retire, that you could just quit whatever work it was the Lord had allowed you to put your hand to, kick back in a lawn chair with a beer and never hit a lick at a snake again.

But the truth still in the husk was that Viola Tackett yearned to stop clawing and scratching. Longed to ride easy. Life *owed* her that. She'd got stomped on hard and she was determined to collect payback — with interest. Going hungry night after night when she's a little kid, the ache in her belly so constant her jaw was always sore from gritting her teeth. She and her brother Lester had beat Joey Purdom with a stick for the candy bar the preacher'd left and Joey wasn't never right in the head after. When Lester tried to keep more than half, she'd broke his arm to get her fair share. For nigh on to seven decades she'd watched *other people* get what she wanted but couldn't have — *stuff*, big houses, fancy cars and the like. She never let on to nobody she gave a rat fart about such as that. She'd learned early and well you didn't never let folks know what really mattered to you 'cause they'd snatch it away. But she *did* care. Oh my, yes, indeedy she shore did. She coveted an easy life with fine things and folks doin' for her and makin' over her.

But for all her scramblin' lo these many years, she was still sitting in the weeds on the side of the road, watchin' *other folks* drive by in a car they didn't have to worry wasn't gonna make it to wherever it was they was going. She was looking the end of life square in the eye, the last of the sand was drainin' out of the hourglass and it was now or never. It was her turn, and wasn't *nothin'* Viola Tackett wouldn't do to grab hold of what was due her.

Her boys helped, best as they could. Neb, Obie and Zach, they was good boys, done whatever she told them to do, but dad-gum if wasn't all of them dumb as fire hydrants. She'd often pondered on what it was that'd made them so, like might be it was from Jack whoring around and he got some kind of disease, but the doctor said no. Said Esther had a thing called Down syndrome and that wasn't something you could catch from a prostitute.

She knew the fault wasn't with her female parts when Malachi come along. Jack didn't know it, of course, but that boy wasn't his git and soon's she had the right kind of seed in her womb, she'd growed a boy there to be proud of. Tall and strong, so good lookin' all the girls was fightin' to drop their drawers for him. He wasn't obedient like the other boys, though. She'd told him he'd ought to drop out of school at sixteen to help his brothers in "the family business." He'd stayed to graduate. After that, she'd *laid down the law* — he was *not* going to go off and join the military. She flat out would *not* have it. And 'course after a while he went on ahead and done it anyway. They packed him off to some place with a name you couldn't pronounce and when he come home, he …

Actually, her Malachi never did come home. Somebody who looked like him, talked like him, walked and liked strawberry pancakes like him come home. But her boy never did. He had got lost out there somewhere in the jungles or desert or wherever it was he went.

No, that wasn't the way of it.

It wasn't that he'd stayed there. He'd come home

alright, but he'd brought that war home with him when he come.

They had a name for it, like giving a thing a name made some kind of difference somehow. Once you knew what to call it, well, everything was gonna be just fine.

PTDS something. Initials. She'd gone to the library in Carlisle right after Malachi got home, looked it up. What she found described what was happening to her boy like somebody'd been standing there watching him, taking notes.

But that's as far as it went. They named it, and after they done that, apparently everybody smiled at each other and shook hands and went home. Didn't nobody say nothing about what to do about it, how to *fix it*. Viola wasn't surprised. Every person she'd ever knowed with nothing more than book smarts was a fool.

Brushing a stray hair out of her face, Viola glanced in the rearview mirror and didn't like the old woman who looked back at her. She'd been a pretty girl, not beautiful by anybody's reckoning, missed it by her features bein' too big and blunt, and by the space between her two front teeth on the top that she never did get fixed and was there to this day.

But the woman who looked back at her now was somebody she had come to know over the passage of years and to understand, but would never fancy. She had a hard face. Not sharp-angles hard. She had round cheeks to go with her dumpy little body and a soft turkey neck under her chin. The hardness was in the eyes, sunk so deep in caverns she sometimes thought they looked like cigarette burns in her face. Even at almost seventy, her hair was still jet black, only had streaks of white through it now, looked like lightning bolts on a night sky. And it still hung all the way to her waist when it wasn't done up in a bun at the back of her neck.

Around her face, her hair had turned pure white, though, like maybe she'd got a good look into hell as she wasn't supposed to see and it'd seared her, left its mark. In them eyes was pain. And rage. The pain of Daddy fooling with her and her sisters ever night soon's it got good dark outside, how he'd take a lantern and set it by the bed cause he wanted to see. Her sisters always cried but Viola never did, never shed one tear, not even when she was squatting by herself in the back of the chicken house, birthing his git, twins, wrung their necks, the both of them 'fore they ever drew a breath. And it'd been Viola who'd took revenge for all of them, though maybe her sisters'd done the same kind of things she done when they had the chance. She'd never asked and they was all dead now so she never would know.

In them eyes was the sound of Elizabeth Mary — her only other little girl — coughing and coughing. And the silence that roared in when the coughing stopped. There was the pain of them tiny coffins, one after the other of them. Just get one settled in the dirt and you'd pick up a baby to nurse and it'd be cold as a rubber doll. Them coffins was always so small she worried the little 'uns wouldn't fit but they always did.

And folks said they was a mean streak in them eyes, too, but they was wrong about that part. Wasn't no *streak* of mean in Viola Tackett. What you seen in them eyes — so dark brown you couldn't hardly see the black spot in the middle — was what you got, and there was *waaaay* more than just a streak of it. Wasn't a single person still drawing breath who could lay claim to crossing Viola Tackett. She always settled her accounts, no matter how long it took, and her books always balanced.

The old truck bounced down into another pothole as she was about to cross into Drayton County and she only had time to wonder about maybe picking some okra to fry for supper when she and the truck fell into a black nothingness that sparkled like black glitter, and her ears filled with a sound like static.

Chapter Three

Nower County Deputy Sheriff Liam Montgomery pulled his cruiser out onto County Road 278 West from the shoulder and flipped on his lights. Not the siren, though. He certainly wasn't an expert on anything having to do with law enforcement, since he didn't even have a year's experience in the position, but it just seemed to him that a siren was *yelling* at people. And he didn't see any sense in yelling unless folks didn't answer when you spoke to them the first time.

The fella who'd taught the handful of night classes in law enforcement that Liam had taken at Eastern Kentucky University in Richmond had stressed how polite you needed to be. He'd said psychological tests demonstrated that people tended to mirror the attitude of the people around them. You needed to speak nice and respectful to the folks you pulled over—

"Hello, ma am, I hate to tell you but you got a tail light's burned out."

If you was being nice, chances are you'd get nice back. But if you put on a "Yore in a heap a'trouble, boy" attitude like you seen in the movies, you'd likely find trouble looking right back at you from the driver's seat.

Of course, Liam wouldn't have been able to pull off anything that macho if he'd tried, cursed as he was with a baby face, round cheeks, curly blond hair and almost no chin at all. Still, roaring up behind somebody with your bubble-gum machine flashing and your siren wailing — Liam seen that as just plain rude. And if he didn't have to be rude, he wouldn't be.

But the fella driving the car with Pennsylvania plates was either blind or thought if he ignored the flashing lights behind him and just kept going, the officer would think of some other more important thing he needed to do and leave him alone and not give him a ticket for *going eighty-five in a fifty-five-mile zone*.

Liam reached up and flipped on his siren as he approached the sign the chamber of commerce put up that welcomed folks into the county on one side and told them goodbye on the other.

"Ya'll come back now, hear."

The boards of the sign were sagging, the paint chipped. Liam was surprised last night's storm hadn't done what years of neglect had failed to do. Though it looked ready to collapse, it still stood beside the road about half a mile from the county line, and if the guy from Pennsylvania didn't pull over in that half mile, Liam'd have all kind of paperwork to do with the Beaufort County Sheriff's Department. When he passed the sign, he caught sight of the other side in his rearview mirror. Even backwards, he knew what it said. It told you everything you needed to know.

"Welcome to Nower County, Kentucky." That's what it was *supposed* to say. But years ago, some vandals, most likely drunk teenagers, had taken red paint and added two letters to "Nower." They stuck a big red *H* between the "w" and the "e" and added another "E" to the end of the word. Then the sign read:

"Welcome to Now***H***er***E*** County, Kentucky."

They'd done the same thing to every one of the welcome signs on all the county roads and as far as Liam knew, nobody had ever made any attempt to change the signs back. It was, after all, just calling a spade a spade. Nower County might have been somewhere once. Before the factory closed. Before the new Bluegrass Parkway was routed through Beaufort instead of Nower County. Before they closed the high school and the elementary school, the hospital and nursing home. Before the incorporated township of Persimmon Ridge had un-incorporated itself and most of the stores on Main Street had closed.

There were a handful of un-incorporated areas that still had a business or two. He'd waved a hidey-do to Dr. E.J. Hamilton when he passed him on the way to work this morning at the crossroads. If the story was true — and wasn't no reason to believe it wasn't — the intersection of Route 17 and County Road 278 was the geographic center of Nower County.

A little strip mall had tried to happen on the north side of County Road 278 at the crossroads back in the day but wasn't much left of it now. E.J.'s Healthy Pets Veterinary Clinic and Animal Hospital was the only functioning enterprise there. It was a going concern, but beyond it were four boarded-up store fronts. The Dollar General Store sat in a building of its own next to the clinic.

There was a bus shelter at the bottom of the parking lot about fifty feet back up County Road 278 from the intersection, though bus service into the county had been discontinued decades ago. The roof over the metal bench was held up by walls on both ends that were so covered in graffiti now it was hard to see through the panes of plexi-glass. It sat beneath a lone streetlight with a white hood rusted almost completely through.

About fifteen years ago, some enterprising citizen had affixed a professional-looking sign on that light pole proclaiming the area to be the "Middle of Nowhere," with one of those little "You Are Here" icons at the bottom.

Nobody ever took that sign down either, and it was likely because it had seemed clever at first. The geographic center of NowHerE County ... the Middle of Nowhere. Get it? Ha. Ha.

But as life hustled by out there in the rest of the world and droned on in insignificance here, folks didn't change the signs because they figured they were accurate. This was Nowhere County and they were nowhere people. Simple as that.

The speeder blew past the county line into Beaufort County with Liam only fifty yards behind, light flashing, siren screaming.

And then the world went black. Black but not dark. Sparkling black. Liam caught a final glimpse of the car with Pennsylvania plates flying off into the blackness before everything was gone and a buzzing filled his head.

Chapter Four

Holmes Fischer — Fish to his friends, and most everybody he'd ever met fell into that category — wasn't certain how he'd gotten here, or where exactly "here" was. He was certain, however, that he had just enough booze in him to comb the tangles out of his nerves but not nearly enough to make the world fuzzy and the memories go away. He was getting there, though. At least he thought he was, if he could just figure out ...

Trying to piece together his fragmented thoughts was like trying to assemble one of those 1,000-piece jigsaw puzzles. Work on it really hard and eventually you might be able to get the edges straight, but all the stuff in the middle was still a jumble, and you couldn't help wondering how many pieces were lying on the floor or under the couch, critical pieces without which the puzzle would never be complete. That also served as a convenient out, when the pieces wouldn't fit together and you were flat-out tired of fooling with it — well, there was a piece missing, that's all.

He found himself about to quote out loud a line from

King Lear about … But he stopped. He had almost broken himself of that habit. You couldn't go around in Nowhere County, Kentucky quoting Shakespeare and still be accepted by the populace as a not-dangerous vagrant. And he definitely didn't want the good folks to decide he was mental, that he needed institutionalizing instead of just another stiff drink. If that happened, they'd ship him off on an all-expenses paid trip to Saint Somebody's Home for the Bewildered and he did *not* want to spend his last days in a place like that — *sober.*

If he remained for all to see sane, then he could continue in the lifestyle he had chosen as the county's homeless man who wasn't homeless. Well, technically, he was homeless, that being defined by Merriam-Webster as a person without a home. But if you wiggled the edges of the definition just a little bit, stretched it spandex-style to fit a bigger set of hips, then he was more accurately described as multi-homed. On Monday nights, he usually slept in the basement of the Methodist church. He could still let himself in even though the church had folded and the minister'd run off with the only valuable item the church owned — a computer. Though its only riches were long gone, the doors were still locked, but he knew where the key was, and the teenagers contented themselves with vandalizing the sanctuary, spray painting the walls and throwing a pew through the stained glass window, and left his humble abode alone. Had a cot, even a hot plate that had worked until the electric company cut the power to the building.

On Tuesdays, he laid down his head on the screened-in porch of Miss Wilimena Crandle, who always left blankets, usually left something to eat or drink, a sandwich or a coke cola. And even once in a blue moon, she'd leave a beer.

He had residences like that all over the county. Transportation between them was the only challenge, as it had apparently been last night or he would not have awakened this morning with dew on his jacket and a fragrant mimosa tree blocking his view of the sunrise.

His wasn't a bad life, he reminded himself, even if right now he couldn't recall exactly where he had been going or why. Particularly on a beautiful spring Friday. Or Saturday. Definitely one or the other, in June. He was sure about the June part, a couple of days in, the third or fourth. And the year — 1995.

Kentucky was beautiful in the springtime, when the azaleas were in full bloom, blossoms so heavy they weighed the limbs down to the ground. Pink and white dogwood trees. Cherry blossoms in the tree at the front gate of the cemetery, under whose boughs he had spent more than a few nights, cuddled up warm in a sleeping bag that Lester Peetree at the hardware store had gifted him. He kept it inside the Mason family's crypt.

Lester had been a good student, seemed to really enjoy Fish's literature class when he was a sophomore. Fish had let him read the part of the narrator in *Our Town* when the class did a reading enactment of the play the year before …

Ah, yes. Before. There was Before. And there was After. And never the twain shall meet, so let it be written, so let it be done. Fish needed a drink.

And that's where he'd been going, said a little memory that bubbled to the top of his awareness, like those little bubbles from the aerator in a fish tank, coming slowly up to the top to vanish. Fish had been on his way to that liquor store a few miles inside the Beaufort County line. Nowhere County was dry. Could you beat that. That's what you got when a bunch of Baptists got hold of a place. Oh, that didn't mean the county residents didn't drink. Of course, they did. It was just inconvenient, that's all. They could get beer at Henderson's Grocery Store, but hard liquor — particularly, Fish's favorite Maker's Mark bourbon — was only available if you crossed the county line. He had never come up with the right adjective to describe the line of cars with Nowhere County plates in front of that store's drive-in window on a Friday night. Pathetic, maybe. Sad, certainly. Hypocritical — absolutely that, too.

He had been on his way to Saunders Wine and Spirits in an unincorporated area in Beaufort County just on other side of the Nowhere County line. It being the last day of the month, he would have money in his account by the time the check he was about to write cleared, so he could purchase legal alcohol. In a few weeks, he'd be buying cheap moonshine wherever he could get it and cough syrup from the Dollar Store when he couldn't, but he always treated himself to some decent whiskey when his retirement check from the Kentucky Teacher's Association came in at the first of the month.

That's where he'd been going. Now see, he *had* been able to put some of the pieces together after all. Not enough for a full picture, of course, but he had no desire for a complete picture. Not seeing a full picture was most of the point in drinking, after all.

He got to his feet. The ground all around was wet but the pile of pine boughs he'd been sleeping on had kept him dry. He wasn't even cold, but that was the booze, not the pine needles. Dusting off his coat and pants, he relieved himself behind the trunk of a persimmon tree and made his way down the embankment and back up onto the shoulder of the road. He would hitch a ride if he could get one. Why had he ridden only far enough to see the "Wel-come to Nowhere County" sign and then ended up in the woods sleeping off his inebriation under a tree? Who had he hitched a ride with and why had they let him out …? There'd been a storm with wind that buffeted the car, knocked tree limbs across the road in front of it. They'd stopped because you couldn't drive in a wind like that. And then …

No, those pieces were obviously under the table, maybe kicked into the footsie and fur-ball enclave of darkness under the couch. Where he was indeed loath to seek them out. To what end? He often had no idea how he had been transported to a given location. What difference did it make?

When he stepped up onto the shoulder of the road, he saw a car fly by clearly going too fast, as evidenced by the red lights and siren trailing behind it like the tail on a kite. The county-mounty in hot pursuit was Liam Montgomery. Fish waved but Liam didn't respond.

Both cars went around the bend out of sight and Fish started walking, his back to oncoming traffic, his hand out with his thumb up. Somebody'd pick him up and take him to the store. Or they wouldn't, in which case he would walk.

The morning was warm. He felt sweat bead on his brow and considered taking off his jacket. But he'd made it a practice over the years to keep his jacket on — otherwise he would leave it somewhere and have to figure out a way to come by a new one. He rounded the corner where the vehicles had disappeared from sight and approached the Beaufort County line.

He stumbled a little, lost his footing, but didn't go all the way down. When he looked back up again he saw himself coming toward him.

That was crazy. He stopped cold in his tracks, looking. About ten feet in front of him was a mirror. Why in the name of all things reasonable in the world was there a mirror out here stretching across the road? It was a mirror, after all, though even squinting to clear his vision, he couldn't see the frame of the mirror, or what was holding it upright. He approached his reflection, noted that his coat was ripped, the sleeve of it. He needed to get that fixed. He'd ask Martha Whittiker to sew it up for him and likely she'd tell him it was not fit to be repaired and get him one of her husband's old jackets that were still hanging in the bedroom closet ten years after he died.

Fish took another step toward the mirror. Got a really good look at the hollows of his face, the scraggly beard, the empty eyes. He never looked in the mirror. When he shaved, and that wasn't often, he only looked at his cheeks and the lather and the razor scraping along the skin. He didn't look at his whole face. Probably hadn't really looked at himself in …

He didn't know.

But he was looking now, at the bright sky-blue eyes that had faded to an overcast day. At the mouth with loose lips. The hairs growing out of his nose. His whole body so skinny he could have played the part of the superstitious Ichabod Crane in *The Legend of Sleepy Hollow*, a priggish school teacher he had strived his whole career *not* to emulate.

He didn't like seeing himself, didn't like having that image planted in his brain so that when he thought of himself that's what he'd see. He much preferred the no-longer-accurate but infinitely more pleasing image of himself as the thin young man who taught high school English by day and by night expanded his consciousness with mushrooms and peyote and psychedelic drugs that opened up for his inspection and enjoyment an unknown alternative universe of extraordinary beings …

That was before.

This was after. After he discovered the beings weren't imaginary. After he came to understand they waited for him in the mist.

The man with hollow eyes and only a finite number of days left to run from reality in this world, as evidenced by the sallow skin, the tremble in his hands, and the way his coat hung on him, not like a coat hanger but like a scarecrow.

That's another part he could play. The scarecrow in *The Wizard of Oz*. But he wasn't out looking for a brain. He had a perfectly good brain, thank you very much. A functioning brain. A brain that he did everything within his power to dull, pack in cotton, soak in a haze of inebriation. He would not ask the Wizard for a brain. Oh no, no, no. If he ever encountered the "whiz of a wiz if ever a wiz there was," he would ask the man pulling levers behind the curtain to take the brain he already had. He'd ask the wizard to leave his head empty, so vacant there weren't even dust bunnies on the floor. Then he would pack the empty head full of straw.

He put out his hand, as his image put out its hand, and when their fingers touched the whole world went black, but he could see in the blackness as if it were light. Fish heard a sound that … No, he didn't hear it. You hear with your ears, not with your fingers and your navel and your elbow. Not with your whole body. And he heard the static-y sound with every cell in his body, a mighty, fuzzy, buzzing sound that filled up his whole being, so loud-but-not-loud it loosened one of his fillings.

The dark and the sound ate up his world.

Chapter Five

Sam Sheridan was a big girl. Oh, not heavy. All long arms and legs as a child, she grew up to be slender and willowy — and to stand just over six feet tall in flat-heeled shoes, and she *always* wore flats. Her height had propelled her into the prestigious starting center spot on the Nower County High School girls' basketball team back in the day. Some of the best memories of her life came from that time, the thump-thump of the ball on the hardwood, the sound of shoes squeaking, and the smell of girl sweat and deodorant and damp hairspray. The "thrill of victory and the agony of defeat." That kind of thing. And she'd felt in control of her life then, strong and competent, in a way she had not felt since.

Look out, world
You best run
We're the class of '81

Two more classes graduated from the school before they closed it down and bussed the kids into Carlisle in

24

Beaufort County to a regional high school. Two years after that, they'd done the same thing with the elementary school — the year before Rusty was supposed to start kindergarten they'd shut the place down.

When Sam had graduated, the name "Martha Ann Sheridan" was printed on the diploma. In first grade, somebody'd noticed that the initials MAS backwards was SAM. So "Sam" had happened and stuck. After high school, life had happened, and Rusty — *Russell!* — had happened, and her waitress job at the Me N' Todd's Whistle Stop Cafe and Grill was in danger of becoming her career path to ... well, to nowhere. But she saw that one coming and dodged the bullet. Though she'd never said as much to anybody except her best friend in elementary school, Sam had always dreamed of becoming a doctor. That wasn't going to happen to the fourth child of eight in the family of an often out-of-work coal miner. She downshifted her sights to registered nurse, RN. Then downshifted again. She'd had to scratch and claw her way through night school, but she'd managed to earn her LPN — became a Licensed Professional Nurse, which had landed her the position as the home health care nurse with the State Department of Human Resources for the tri-county area that included Nower, Beaufort and Drayton counties.

It was that job that had sent Sam to the Dollar General Store at the crossroads this morning. On your feet all day, you better have the right kind of shoes. She splurged on shoes when she asked for no other luxuries. New Balance Women's WC806 D-width tennis shoes — size 10 — that cost almost $75 at Landon's Shoe Store in Carlisle. They might be cheaper somewhere in Lexington, but Sam didn't have time to chase all over Lexington looking for shoes. Her New Balance were strictly for work, which was why she'd come to the Dollar General Store this morning to pick up a pair of cheaper Adidas or Fila to wear when she mowed the grass.

Rusty's Air Jordans had similar restricted use and he was scrupulously careful with them. The boy would go barefoot before he'd wear an off brand — what he called buddy shoes — to school.

Tall wasn't Sam's only striking attribute, though it was the one that suited her personality best. When she was waiting tables, she had zero tolerance for men who couldn't keep their hands to themselves and being bigger than most of them helped her set up what she called her *boundary of respect.* Every man who had ever dared to cross that boundary had been very, very sorry he had.

She had an open, inviting face with a high wide forehead, just shy of pretty, though a big smile tipped the scales, and she was seldom without one of those. Her voice was surprisingly husky, kind of a startling rumble, that made her memorable — if her height and strawberry blonde hair hanging straight almost to her waist hadn't already chiseled her image into your psyche.

The shopping basket she'd picked up by the Dollar General Store front door was almost filled by the big shoe box. She should have gotten a cart because a stop at the Dollar Store always awakened the tiny voices of a whole list of sorta-kinda necessary items all shouting in unison in their tinny voices, *"pick me, pick me!"*

Dishwashing detergent. When she'd squeezed the bottle last night over the frying pan, nothing had come out but a dribble of blue liquid and bubbles. Steak sauce. She didn't use it on steak, of course, but Rusty loved to put it on Spam.

Rusty. That reminded her. The boy needed socks — white tube socks with the stripes at the top always in different colors so you eventually had a pile of lone soldiers in the unmatched-sock sack.

Toilet paper. She had several rolls, but standing before her in a huge display were bundles of six — on sale. No reason not to stock up. Far as she could remember, she'd never had a roll of toilet paper go bad on her.

Gummy bear vitamins. Not for Rusty, for Sam! Hair scrunchies that the magazine in the dentist's office waiting room proclaimed were woefully out of vogue but she had to have something to keep all that hair out of her face. Flashlight batteries — or buy candles. One or the other. She passed on the display billed as a "bigger, better mouse-trap," though the one she used now was the laughingstock of the whole mouse population of the county.

Her basket was full to overflowing when she started to the checkout counter and when a packet of tube socks made a break for it, taking a swan dive off the top of the shoebox, the resulting avalanche was unpreventable.

Abigail Clayton appeared at Sam's side and began helping her pick up what she'd dropped.

Abby was Sam's physical opposite. Where Sam was tall and lithe and moved with the grace of a former athlete, Abby was short and as boney/frail as a baby bird that didn't yet have feathers. Her shock of unruly hair was an untamable mass of curly frizz a color Sam's mother would have dubbed dishwater blonde.

She handed Sam the shoebox containing the size-ten sneakers.

"I could about put both my feet in one of them shoes," she said, indicating the maybe-a–size-five feet on the ends of her skinny white legs. She was wearing pink plastic flip-flops. One bore the face of Beauty and the other of the Beast from the children's movie. "I mostly wear kids' shoes. They fit fine and they're cheaper than grownup sizes."

The girl's face still bore a red flush from the adolescent acne that had made her skin look like ground meat only a couple of years ago. She was nobody's definition of attractive, but she was beautiful today, totally beaming.

"Lordy, girl, the glow on your face is warm enough to melt frost off a windowpane," Sam said, and the smile Sam would have bet couldn't possibly get wider did — so wide across the bottom of Abby's face if the ends connected in the back, the top of her head would fall off.

"I got ever-thing in the world to smile 'bout. Gonna be bringing my Cody home this mornin'."

That *was* big news.

Abby had grown up so far back in some hollow the sun probably didn't shine there more than a couple of days a week. Her father was a disabled coal miner and Sam had no idea how many brothers and sisters she had — but it was a bunch. She did know that the oldest, Claude, was locked up somewhere in a mental hospital, judged incompetent to stand trial for hacking his druggie roommates to death with a meat cleaver.

Abigail Letcher and Shepherd Clayton quit school at sixteen — the legal age to do so, and almost seventy percent of the high school students availed themselves of that privilege — and got married. They moved into a little rental house off Swords Creek Road in Poorfolk Hollow that at least had running water. No indoor plumbing, though, literally didn't have "a pot to piss in," but they were young and stupid and didn't know their circumstances should have made them miserable. Sam knew Abby's story because one of her many sisters cut Sam's hair at the Hair Affair Beauty Parlor and Nail Salon on Main Street in Carlisle.

"She was so excited when she got pregnant you'd have thought she's the first female on the face of the earth ever had a baby," her sister Ramona had said, as she ran Sam's wet hair through her fingers and told Sam for the umpteen-billionth time how she'd trade out her black hair for Sam's red any day. "Then she got that pre-something."

Pre-eclampsia. That had put her to bed, and Shep'd had to cut his work hours back as far as they'd let him at the storm-door factory in Lexington, which was an hour-and-a-half commute from Nower County. Abby had become one of Sam's circuit of home-bound patients for a time, and then the baby came early, had what Ramona called "all kind of preemie troubles," and the child remained for several months in the hospital's neonatal unit — while the couple racked up medical debt, the numbers getting bigger and bigger every day, faster than the numbers on a gasoline pump when you fill up the tank.

"This here's the first time I been home in two months, spent ever day and ever night with Cody. But Shep's with him now and I come home to get his room all ready."

She grinned, displaying crooked teeth that had likely never been in the presence of a dentist.

"Shep sent me home to get a good night's sleep in my own bed last night because I ain't likely to be getting much sleep from now on. Cody being so little and all, you got to feed him ever two hours 'round the clock."

She looked suddenly shy.

"I been, you know, pumpin' … feeding it to him outa a bottle because at first he was too weak to suck. But this morning when I get there, I ain't gonna be giving him that last bottle. I'm gonna *nurse* him. Nurse my baby for the first time."

That *was* special. Sam remembered nursing Rusty.

"Shoot, I might as well have gone on back to the hospital when I got done last night because I didn't sleep a wink."

"Yeah, that was some storm!" Sam had never seen anything like it.

"Oh, wasn't the storm kept me awake. Just, you know, the jitters. I would have got in the truck and went on back but I told my sister Eva Joan I'd stop by on my way up Lexington this morning — she lives in Frogtown so it ain't much out of the way — to fetch them cloth diapers she's been collecting for me. Me and Shep can't afford them disposables."

"Good thing you wasn't lookin' to buy no diapers here," said the bored teenage checker, who needed to wash her hair and stop snapping her bubble gum. "We ain't got none. Delivery truck didn't show up this morning."

Abby put the pack of preemie onesies on the checkout counter.

"Pour little thing ain't got no clothes that fit — even these preemies is too big, but I'm gonna fatten him up quick as I can, nurse him ever ten minutes if that's what he wants." She opened her purse and pulled from it a little snap-shut change purse, withdrawing some folded bills and flattening them on the counter.

"Enjoy him while he's little," Sam told her. "Before you know it, you won't be able to snap those around his fat little butt. You ever need a babysitter, give me a call."

"Shoot, I ain't gonna be leaving him nowhere. Once I finally get my hands on that baby, I might not put him down long enough for him to learn to walk."

Abby went out the door, jingling the bell, and the checker was only half through ringing up Sam's order when Abby came running back in.

"You got to come help!" Her voice was breathless and frightened. "They's a woman out on the bench there, sick, puking her guts up, and a little girl's sitting beside her with blood running down her face. Something's bad wrong."

Chapter Six

Charlie blinked but her vision was so blurred she closed her eyes again. That's when the nausea hit her. From out of nowhere, she was suddenly so sick to her stomach she was barely able to lean over in time to keep from spewing a noxious puddle of this morning's toast, jelly and coffee into her own lap.

She heaved and heaved, the kind of sick you get from the worst hangover you ever had, the kind that makes your diaphragm muscles strain.

She heaved so violently she could barely get her breath, and all the while she heard a pulsing sound that didn't really seem like a sound because she didn't think she was hearing it with her ears. It seemed like the sound was inside her head, bouncing around from one side to the other like a tennis ball in an empty oil drum.

WHUM!
WHUM!
WHUM!

The rhythm seemed to be keeping time with her heaving and gasping.

She was unaware of her surroundings until she finally got her breath, gasped and tried to choke off the next wave of heaving.

The sound in her head gradually subsided to a steady *Whum. Whum. Whum.* Then *whumwhumwhum.* Softer, a background, the canvas on which emerging reality was painted.

It was hot. She was sitting in the sun, and when she looked up she had to squeeze her eyes shut and turn away.

Then she heard Merrie's voice, her tear-clotted voice, the sound of a child who has been crying for a long time. Charlie almost shook her head to get her bearings, but didn't. She was absolutely positive that her entire skull was filled with blown glass, some kind of fragile crystal, thinner than an egg shell. Any sudden movement of it would …

Just thinking about a sudden movement could shatter it.

Everything was all wrong.

What was happening?

In an accident? A wreck?

Voices were speaking to her and she opened her squinty eyes.

Bad move. The world heaved and swayed when she did and the people leaning over her took on the proportions of images in a funhouse mirror.

People standing over her.

Where was she?

Where …?

She made herself open her eyes, made herself focus and discovered that fighting the vertigo and nausea helped to alleviate it.

There was a red-haired woman standing in front of her.

Where was she?

What is … where are …?

She couldn't order words in her head enough to speak. Then someone called her name, part of it.

"… Charlie Ryan, aren't you? Remember me, Sam Sheridan?"

And then reality slammed down around her, the finality of a prison cell door banging shut.

She was sitting on a bench — somewhere … and Merrie was sitting beside her, crying.

Merrie!

Her mind snapped back into focus, a rubber band stretched to the limit and set free.

Merrie had tripped and hit her head. She was bleeding. Charlie had strapped her into the car seat and …

That was it. The memories were gone after that, wiped clean.

She must have been in some kind of wreck … an accident.

Merrie was crying a listless sort of cry. There was enough dried blood on her face to indicate she'd either been attacked by an ax murderer, or had been an extra on the set of *The Texas Chainsaw Massacre*.

Though most of the blood was dry, there was an oozing wound under a crude bandage on her forehead.

Charlie had put the bandage on. Had done the best she could to secure it, but there'd been only Band-Aids, no surgical tape, nothing to hold it to the wiggling, wailing child before she strapped the little girl into the car seat to take her—

She'd been on her way to the hospital, to the emergency room. And then …

Again, nothing.

"… need to get her stitched up …" a voice said.

She attended to the last, looked … really *looked* at the

people around her. A woman with long, strawberry blonde hair blowing daintily in the breeze was down on one knee in front of Merrie, carefully examining the bandage. There was a skinny blonde woman there and an overweight teenage girl, but those two weren't standing near her, and it was clear why. She had puked all over the ground around her. The smell of it caused nausea to roll back in, a wave stretching out up a sandy beach.

"Can you hear me, Charlie? Do you understand?"

That was the red-headed woman who looked familiar but Charlie couldn't place her. Her voice was husky, low and soothing.

"We need to see to the little girl's cut."

Now there was somebody speaking sense.

"Yes, stitches. That's where I was going when …"

Yeah, when what?

"Where am I?" She hated how much that sounded like every groggy heroine in every cheap movie who wakes up after fill-in-the-blank and can't remember which guy she went home with.

But *where was she?*

"At the crossroads," said the young woman with blonde hair and bad teeth.

"The Middle of Nowhere," said the redhead who—

"*Sam?* Sam Sheridan?"

Charlie was surprised she was able to pull that name out of the memory banks because she surely had not laid eyes on the woman since the night of graduation from high school. Sam had played basketball.

Sam nodded, then asked, "What happened to your little girl?"

Reality was settling more permanently around her.

"She fell, tripped over a fallen limb in the driveway of

her grandmother's house. I was taking her to the emergency room when …"

She looked around.

"Where's my car?"

The people standing in front of her all had the same I-got-no-idea-lady look on their faces.

Sam was taking over and that was a good thing because right now Charlie needed someone taking over.

"E.J.'s office is right there." Sam pointed to the building next to the Dollar General Store. "He's got supplies. We can clean her up, get that wound properly bandaged."

E.J. … the name. Elijah Hamilton.

Sam had already gotten Merrie to her feet and she held her hand out to help Charlie to hers.

"I can butterfly it, make a sterile bandage. Or he can put in some stitches … and not have to worry that his patient's going to bite him."

Elijah Hamilton. A veterinarian.

She burped out a bleat of inappropriate laughter but couldn't help it. A veterinarian. She'd been upset she couldn't take Merrie to a pediatric plastic surgeon instead of an ordinary emergency room doctor and this woman was suggesting she let a guy who neutered dogs sew up the wound.

But she allowed herself to be helped to her feet, and didn't protest because a person really needed to be in much more control of themselves, their faculties, and their memories to exert authority and Charlie was totally confused.

She had at least reverted to default mothering mode. She felt steady enough on her feet that she reached down and picked Merrie up into her arms.

"We're gonna get you fixed right up, sweetie pie," she

said and Merrie nodded but said nothing. She no longer had a blank stare, but she wasn't engaging with the world either.

Sam Sheridan led the little parade across the Dollar General Store parking lot toward the building with a sign proclaiming Healthy Pets Veterinary Clinic and Animal Hospital.

"You don't need my help no more and I got to be going," said the blonde woman. "Gonna be late as it is."

"I'm good, Abby, thanks. Hug that little one for me."

The young woman was homely, had the stamp of ancestors who hadn't been particular about marrying their cousins. But she looked momentarily beautiful, her face wrapped in a joy that some people never achieved in a lifetime. "I shore will."

She turned and headed toward an old pickup truck parked in front of the Dollar General Store, followed by the teenager, who had not said a word, merely went into the store.

Charlie could tell that Sam had a lot of questions she wanted to ask, but she was wisely not asking any of them. Charlie instantly liked her for that. No, she *recovered* affection for her from a well long forgotten.

Sam opened the door of the veterinary clinic for Charlie carrying Merrie, and in the reflection in the window on the door Charlie noticed that the sign was still there on the light pole in the parking lot. The words were backwards, but she didn't need to be able to read it to know what it said.

The Middle of Nowhere.

Chapter Seven

Charlie wasn't drunk, though that was the go-to explanation for sitting in a public bus shelter at nine o'clock in the morning, puking your guts out.

Helping the bleeding little girl had taken precedence in Sam's mind over figuring out the level of sobriety of the child's mother, and there was something wrong with the little girl, too.

She had a wound on her forehead that had been amateurishly bandaged, using only Band-Aids. It was just oozing now, but it appeared to be a typical minimal-damage, maximum-bleeding head wound. The child's face and her Whitney Houston tee-shirt were bloodstained. Tears had traced twin tracks of clean through the dried blood on her cheeks.

But the thing was, the little girl looked like a zombie. The child should have been sobbing but she wasn't. She was crying an energy-less cry, like she'd learned how from a manual, and otherwise was mostly unresponsive. She'd been just sitting there, staring sightlessly, crying her robot cry, while her mother made violent retching sounds next to her on the bench.

Both of them seemed to be the kind of dazed you experienced when the airplane you're on crashes and you're the only two survivors. But there was no plane, and no vehicle either, for that matter. Which, of course, begged the question: where did they come from and how had they gotten to the bus shelter? The only vehicle in the parking lot of the Dollar General Store was hers. The disengaged teenage checker must have parked behind the building or had been dropped off at work.

The two came back to reality gradually. The little girl's thousand-yard stare began to fade. The woman started to try to control her vomiting. And none of it had anything to do with Sam's efforts to get through to them. They were … it was like they were waking up, coming back out from under anesthesia, maybe.

When the woman finally lifted her head, Sam recognized her.

Charlene Ryan. Charlie. She and Sam had graduated from high school together. As far as she could remember, Sam hadn't seen her since. And never saw much of her in high school. But in elementary school … the two of them had been inseparable, brought their dolls to school every day. They'd sit in the shade, leaning up against the brick wall during recess "playing babies." Sam wasn't sure if that was before the era of Barbie dolls, but even if it hadn't been, it didn't matter. Both of them wanted to be the mommies of babies — twins and triplets, preferably. The more the merrier.

Charlie was totally disoriented and appeared to be quite sick, but she wasn't drunk. Sam knew drunk. There was no smell of booze, and besides, she wasn't the drunk kind of disoriented. She was the trauma kind of disoriented, which again, begged the questions where had she come from, how did she get here and why?

Which all were questions that could wait. The little girl needed somebody to tend to that wound. And E.J. was right here. Oh sure, he was a veterinarian, but he was certainly a proficient surgeon. She could put a butterfly bandage on it and a dressing until Charlie could get the little girl to a hospital, or E.J. could put in stitches.

Abby had begged off. She needed to get to the hospital and it was a long drive. Sam hollered after the teenager as she went back into the Dollar General that she'd be back later to pick up her purchases, but the kid hadn't even turned around.

"You two just sit and I'll go talk to E.J."

There was no one else in the waiting room until Mrs. Throckmorton — who always put Sam in mind of Tweety Bird's grandmother — came in with her fat Persian cat as Sam was explaining to Raylynn Bennett, the receptionist, what their problem was. Raylynn said E.J. was in with a Rottweiler right now "and you *don't* want to interrupt him, but I'll tell him you're here."

Sam came back to sit beside Charlie as Mrs. Throckmorton told Raylynn, "I'll just take Mittens on back," and went through the door leading into the interior of the clinic.

"I don't know," Charlie said quietly.

"Know what?"

"Anything. I don't know how … I was driving down the road with my screaming daughter in her car seat on the way to the hospital in Beaufort and then …"

"You were in a wreck? Ran off the road?"

"No, I wasn't in a …" She stopped, backtracked. "I don't know what I was in or wasn't in or … none of this makes sense." She shuddered. "And why was I so sick?"

She went pale at the word.

"I've never felt nausea like that. Like I … my stomach was in a terrible hurry to … it was *overwhelming.*" She stopped again. "And last I checked, car wrecks don't usually cause … why was I so sick?"

Sam had a sudden uneasy feeling, fleeting, there and then gone. A sense that something had shifted somewhere, that the seconds that stacked up on the other side of this moment had been knocked off center and would never line up with what had come before.

Raylynn said E.J. could see them and led them to an examining room where the examining table had a metal, tray-like top rather than the human kind with the miles of white paper in a roll stretching out across it.

"Hey Sam, what can I do for you?" E.J. said, and gave her a hug and a peck on the cheek, then turned to Charlie and her little girl. "Raylynn said you—" She watched recognition spread across his face. *"Charlie?"*

Until that moment, Sam had not thought about the fact that E.J. seemed older than they were when in fact he was the same age. He'd always been boney, scarecrow skinny, but it was his hair, or the lack of it, that was the issue. He'd started losing it in his early twenties and now all that remained was a soap ring above his ears and a chrome dome. If he'd done the sexy thing and shaved his head to hide it — and chucked the rimless granny glasses parked on his nose — he'd have looked younger. But maybe it was all right with him to slide into middle age in his early 30s.

Charlie smiled a vague smile, still seemed like she wasn't firing on all her mental cylinders.

"Good to see you, E.J. How are you?" But she didn't wait for him to answer, just nodded to her little girl. "She fell over a tree branch lying in the driveway and cut her head. And I was on the way to …"

She suddenly seemed about to cry.

"On my way to the emergency room in Beaufort County."

E.J. was clearly confused.

"I don't understand what you're doing—"

"Neither do I!" Charlie was holding onto her emotions by her fingernails. "I was in the car and the next thing I knew I was sitting in the bus shelter puking my guts out and I have no memory of anything in between!" She stopped. "Except static, a buzzing sound like a dial tone and a black light—" She heard herself. "*Black light?* Oh dear God I sound like I was abducted by aliens. That'd be funny if it weren't so …"

Taking a deep, cleansing breath, she said, "Would you please … Sam said you might be willing to look at the cut on Merrie's head. Maybe clean it or put on a proper bandage or something."

"Of course I can," he said in a soothing voice, proper bedside-manner mode, and Sam wondered why a veterinarian needed a bedside manner. Then she thought about the Rottweiler.

E.J. concentrated on the little girl Charlie called "Merrie."

"Merrie, with an 'ie', not Mary," Charlie explained. "Not that anybody but me knows or cares about the difference. Short for Meredith but I was always going to call her Merrie. As in Meriadoc Brandybuck."

"And Pippin — *I* get it."

And Sam absolutely *did* remember the characters from the three books they'd read in Mr. Fischer's high school English class. Most of the class hated *The Lord of the Rings* but Sam had fallen head over heels in love with the story and the characters, as had Charlie … and Malachi Tackett, too, come to think of it. Sam had even tried to get the other girls on the basketball team to learn how to speak Elvish, so they could talk and the other team wouldn't understand. That was a bust.

As E.J. worked, Sam studied Charlie without appearing to stare. She hadn't changed much, was still small, by Sam's definition of small which meant she was a normal-sized woman, probably five-five, and strikingly beautiful, her features perfectly matched. Sam had read that somewhere, that beauty was about symmetry, that the faces of beautiful people were perfectly symmetrical, eyes the same size and shape, eyebrows matching … things like that. Sam definitely didn't make the cut under that definition, not with a lone dimple on her right cheek.

Charlie had the same air of confidence she'd had years ago, a standoffishness that had been universally interpreted in high school as snooty. Sam later recognized it for a maturity the others in the class didn't have until later, when they'd earned it. Sam figured Charlie was that mature in high school because she'd earned it along the way there.

Princess Diana! That was it. Charlie's thick, shiny brown hair was cut in the same hairstyle as the Princess of Wales. A shaggy short look Sam was sure required the regular ministrations of a hairdresser. But in between those visits, all Charlie — and the princess, of course — had to do was wash their hair and shake their heads and it'd dry perfect. At least that's what the hairstyle magazines Sam read in the beauty parlor said.

Charlie was dressed casual — jeans and a plaid shirt, untucked. But it was a studied casual look, one that was accomplished by designer jeans, probably a button-down shirt from Macy's, and the shoes were … what? Ballet shoes? No, something clearly expensive that was made to look like ballet shoes, like Jackie O or Audrey Hepburn would wear. Her nails were perfectly manicured and her only jewelry were diamond stud earrings. Small ones, not ostentatious. Yes sir, Charlie Ryan ... McClintock ... was a picture of casual elegance. Designed to appear spontaneous, the look was as stylishly calculated as Cinderella's dress for the ball.

Sam took particular note of the jewelry Charlie *wasn't* wearing — a wedding band. No rings at all on her left hand, but a ring on her right hand was weighed down by a rock the size of a raisin.

As soon as E.J. and Charlie were engaged in conversation, Sam felt awkwardly unnecessary and started to back up. "I'll wait outside."

"No," Charlie said, too forcefully and she knew it. "I mean ..." She reached out and took Sam's hand. "Would you stay and ..." She looked deeply into Sam's eyes and it felt like some long unused connection was re-fastened. "Something's very, very wrong here. You believe that, don't you?"

That was scary, because some part of Sam *did* know that what had apparently happened to Charlie didn't fit neatly between the fence posts of reality. It was off, outside, different in a way that made Sam uncharacteristically uneasy. She felt a chill go down her spine, dripping like ice water from one vertebra to the next.

Even if she hadn't played dolls with Charlie on the playground every day during recess for years, it would have been clear that the woman standing before her was not mentally unbalanced. Freaked out, yes. Crazy ... not so much.

So if she wasn't nuts, what *had* happened to her? And for reasons she couldn't identify, Sam suddenly did not want to know.

Chapter Eight

You'd think that after all he'd been through, the last thing Malachi Tackett would want was a gun in his hand. You'd think that once he got home, got out of uniform, washed away the filth from his body and the horror from his soul, he would swear off all weapons for the rest of his life. You'd think he'd be sickened by the mere sight of one.

But it felt good.

In fact, nothing at all in his whole life felt good except the rifle.

The only times he ever felt the fear begin to ebb away were times like this morning, out before first light, gliding unseen and unheard through the shadows of the trees, from one to the next, waiting for the first of the dawn bird-songs, eyes adjusted to the dark so he could make out which of the lumps on the tree limbs over his head were clumps of leaves and which ones were squirrels.

He had grown up hunting squirrels in these woods. And deer, wild turkeys, the occasional wild boar and all manner of winged creatures from a brace of doves for supper to a fat duck felled from its spot in the V formation rising up off a pond. Some of his best memories had been made here, the early ones, being a little kid caught up in the smell of damp leaves, the sparkle of diamond-studded dew drops on the lacy spiderwebs.

His father had brought him. His brothers had brought him. But he had lived for the day when he didn't need anybody to accompany him, the day when his father had finally put this .22 rifle in his hands and told him to "skin whatever you git before you bring it home. Yore mama don't want that mess on her back porch."

The boy with an unruly shock of black hair the color of the coal under the mountains and eyes as clear blue as the reflection of the sky in the streams winding through the hollows had grown to manhood with a rifle in his hands.

Even now, even after all he'd seen, Malachi didn't quite feel whole and complete without one. Even after he'd seen the way they were used on human prey.

In truth, most of the Rwandans didn't use guns. Guns killed victims too quickly and ammo was expensive. They preferred to slaughter with the tools at hand, the machetes from the fields, the hunting knives, clubs with nails in them. When they fell upon a hut and massacred the family, sometimes they just used sticks or rocks to beat the occupants to death.

Malachai'd seldom been witness to the actual killing, but usually showed up while the blood was still flowing from severed limbs, before the hearts stopped beating. He'd drawn the short straw. While his buddies from the Gulf War were packed off to Bosnia, he was one of only a hundred combat troops sent to Rwanda to secure the airport there during "the unrest." That's all: just *secure* the airport. No one expected the sudden grassfire of carnage that erupted around them. The violence was swift and staggering. Between April and July, the Hutu tribe butchered more than *750,000* men, women and children from the Tutsi tribe. Three quarters of a million people in just a hundred days. The American soldiers in Rwanda were not tasked with preventing the carnage. But they saw it. Oh, my yes, they did see it for a fact.

There was a movement in the leaves of a sycamore tree just ahead and Malachi froze. He'd already racked a shell into the chamber and he slowly lifted the barrel of the rifle, put his eye to the X3 power scope and sighted on the squirrel, a fat gray one, perched on a limb sixty feet away. His mama'd told him once "squirrels ain't nothing but rats with good PR," and that might be a fact, but he and his brothers had never gone out seeking fat rats for supper.

He hadn't noticed the dawn light growing. Technically, it wasn't "dawn" light, since it'd been dawn hours ago out there on the flat. But the sun didn't crest the top of Beetroot Mountain until right about now and he'd been here waiting for it, watching it cast a glow into the tree shadows. His eyes searched the nearby foliage, looking to see how many of the fat gray squirrel's cousins had shown up for an acorn breakfast this morning.

He lowered the rifle, took a quiet step toward the tree and then another to get a better angle. Then he lifted the barrel again. He had accidentally banged the rifle against the truck door a few days ago and knocked the adjustable scope off its zero, making all his shots low and to the right. He needed to readjust the scope. Until he got around to it, he compensated for that as he aimed. Another step and … he almost lost his balance, stumbled slightly when his boot connected with something on the ground.

Just a rock.

A round, white rock. About the size of a grapefruit.

And images of the soccer balls filled his head. At least that's what he'd thought they were at first. But they were too small to be soccer balls and not the right color. They were balls of some kind, though. The floor of the hut was solid with them, side by side so snug up against each other there was no room in between. Who put balls on the ground in …?

Then he got it. Not balls, skulls.

And not adult skulls. These were too small. These were kids.

He hadn't responded in any way. Nothing. Didn't flinch. Didn't puke all over his boots like the captain did. Showed no indication that it wasn't an everyday occurrence in the life of Corporal Malachi Tackett to see all that remained of a couple of hundred children displayed as household decorations.

He'd seen some of the Rwandan soldiers had teeth necklaces. He didn't let himself know they were teeth when he saw them. They were just white stones, that's all. Of course, he knew what they were same as everybody else did, but if you let yourself know a thing like that … really know it as a human being, as a card-carrying member of the human race, the only possible reasonable response was a horror and outrage so monumental it might just rip your whole soul out of your chest.

Every man dealt with it in whatever way he could. Some guys stayed blind drunk every off moment because as long as you were "on," being a soldier, doing your thing, trying not to get your butt shot off, you could bury the images under "doing the necessary." But when the danger abated, when the adrenaline stopped flowing, when the sun shone and butterflies flew and little kids somewhere in the world were laughing … then it hit you.

You found a way to cope with it or … he didn't know "or what" because he hadn't yet found a way. The leg injury that had sent him back home had taken him away from all the other people in the world who had seen what he'd seen, had been where he'd been, had held onto their own souls with their fingernails.

The shrinks claimed that it had "aborted his healing process."

He didn't know about that. All he did know was that he wasn't in charge of nothing anymore. He was just along for the ride.

Sometimes the ride took him back there to some battle somewhere and he had to fight to stay alive. There was a gaping black hole in the middle of back there in Rwanda where some awful demon dwelled, a horror worse than all the others in a place made out of horror, constructed with one brick of horror stacked up on another until you finally couldn't see over the top anymore. In that black hole was what he'd done or hadn't done — that's all he knew about it — and when he finally saw what it was, it would destroy him.

Sometimes he didn't know where he was, some place in between which wasn't either one of them.

The leaving usually started with something like the white rock. The memories. But this morning he only felt the pain and the sorrow and the fear of … he didn't know what … but he stayed in this world. Kept walking but not rightly hunting. Ignoring the squirrels and the rest of the animals as the woods woke up to a new day.

He headed out toward Bald Knob, on the other side of the county line in Drayton County, for no reason he could have articulated. He came to the clearing where you could see the knob and started out across it but stopped when he felt something splat into his face. Like a raindrop out of the clear blue sky. He looked up and saw then, the blood on the tree limbs. Coating the tree limbs. Another drip hit him on the forehead and one landed on his shoulder.

He heard the rattle of gunfire then, turned from the sound and bolted across the meadow ...

Into darkness. No, it wasn't dark, it was light. It was just that the light was black. And his head filled with a buzzing, static sound.

Chapter Nine

There was no chit-chat, no catching up on each other's lives, no what-have-you-been-doing-since-high-school. There was no conversation at all in the examining room as E.J. carefully removed the makeshift bandage Charlie had affixed to the head of the squirming Merrie before she'd strapped the still-screaming child into the car.

She wasn't screaming now, though. Merrie was as docile as if she'd been drugged. In fact, she was acting like she *had* been drugged, not really focusing when you spoke to her. Answered in monosyllabic grunts and didn't respond in any way to E.J.'s poking and prodding of the surely-it-hurt cut on her head. Her eyelids weren't at half-mast like they got at bedtime, though. She was just … staring. True, it was morning nap time, but under the circumstances, Charlie couldn't imagine Merrie was sleepy. And asleep, Meredith McClintock was comatose. You could pick the child up, throw her over your shoulder in a fireman carry and haul her out of a burning building and she'd sleep right through it. She slept so soundly, in fact,

that Charlie had asked her pediatrician if there was something wrong with her. He'd said he wished *he* could sleep
that sound. Merrie didn't even know there'd been a storm
last night, but when she woke up this morning, her eyes
popped open and she was instantly alert, flitting around in
her cheerful, hummingbird fashion. Her behavior now was
neither, and that weird, somewhere-in-between nether-
world frightened Charlie far more than the bloody
wound did.

"I can sew it up from the underside so it won't leave a
scar," E.J. told her, "but you might prefer to take her
to—?"

"Take her? In what?" Charlie bleated out inappropriate laughter again. "I don't have a car. I … lost mine."
She suddenly felt very tired. "Sure, please, do sew it up. I
don't think I'm going to be taking her anywhere today."

Merrie gradually began to focus, to wiggle. As the last
vestiges of Charlie's nausea were finally passing, Merrie
was starting to whine, to pull away from E.J. Charlie was
thrilled to see the return of her headstrong, maybe-just-a-
little-bit-spoiled three-year-old. In fact, the little girl stuck
out her lip in a pout and was teetering on the edge of
being totally uncooperative until E.J. told her he was going
to make the bandage on her head into a crown. That
brought something resembling a smile to Merrie's face. Of
course, E.J. was now going to have to make good on the
bandage-crown promise or suffer through the mother of all
temper tantrums.

The easing of worry about Merrie freed Charlie to
freak out over what had just happened, and she would have
if she'd had any idea what it was.

She told E.J., and Sam for the second time, all she
knew about the situation, and Sam filled E.J. in on the

condition she'd found Charlie and Merrie in the bus shelter.

Had they been … drugged somehow? Why/by whom/where/how?

Or kidnapped? Where/how/by whom/why?

A car-jacking?

"This is crazy!" Frustration painted incipient hysteria on Charlie words. "I was driving along and then … it's nuts!"

"We'll figure out what happened," Sam told her, and it didn't sound like meaningless assurance. It felt like she believed it. And even if she didn't, Charlie was grateful that she'd made the effort to put on a good show of meaning it. That counted for something.

When E.J. was finished, Charlie realized a couple of things.

One, she couldn't pay him because she had no money, no wallet, no credit cards, no identification — all the human documentation necessary to establish your realness in the world. All that had been in her purse. And her purse was in the floorboard of her car … wherever that was.

He wouldn't have taken payment anyway, was so nice she felt embarrassed to have bothered him … what was there about this to be embarrassed about? None of it was *her* fault.

This was crazy.

"Come on," Sam said. "I'll give you a ride home."

When they stepped out the front door of E.J.'s clinic into the bright morning sunshine they both saw him at the same time. There was a man with a rifle crouched beside the east plexiglass wall of the bus shelter, peeking out around the edge of it as if it were shielding him from enemy fire.

Sam gasped.

"Chai!" she cried.

"What?" Charlie was confused.

"That's Malachi Tackett."

And indeed, it was Malachi Tackett. How could Charlie not have recognized him? Well, duh, maybe because he was dressed in camouflage and looking for all the world like he might shoot anything that moved. Not just that, though. The hollow eyes. The ravaged face wearing a look that somehow managed to communicate terror and fury at the same time.

Malachi Tackett. The boy Charlie had had a crush on since kindergarten. The heart-throb quarterback of the high school football team. The boy who'd been a man at seventeen and made all the other boys seem like children.

Malachi Tackett looked their way, saw them, but clearly didn't recognize them. He appeared to see Merrie, though, because he called out, "Get her to the church with the rest of the kids. We'll set up a perimeter, hold them off as long as we can."

Charlie carefully shoved Merrie behind her, held her out of sight there. When Sam started toward Malachi, she grabbed Sam's arm but Sam shook her off and kept going,

"Chai, what are you doing here?" Sam called out as she rushed across the parking lot toward him. "Where did you—"

"Hit the dirt," he yelled at her. "Down ... *now!*"

Charlie took three steps, grabbed Sam's arm and whispered fiercely as she yanked Sam down into a crouch. "Get down! He's not dragging a full string of fish — can't you see that? He's—"

"Around the other side," he called out to nobody they could see. "They're trying to cut us off." He looked frantically from right to left and when he saw Sam start to rise, he cried, "Stay down. You trying to get your head blown off?"

He seemed to make some kind of decision, straightened and took a deep breath.

"I'm going to draw their fire. On my signal, you—"

The voice of the old man surprised them all. "You'll want to put that rifle away now, son," he said and all their eyes yanked to him. Nobody'd noticed his slow approach, leaning heavily on a cane as he made his way across the Dollar General Store parking lot, a mutt that looked to be about as old as he was at the end of a leash beside him. The man had a shaggy beard, bushy mustache and gentle eyes that radiated a thoughtful calm beneath his overgrown eyebrows, and that calm in the tension was as soothing as a cup of hot chocolate on a cold morning.

Malachi Tackett had the drop on everybody over an expanse of vacant concrete without so much as an ant hill for cover. And if the look in his eye was any indication, right now Malachi was crazier than a nuclear waste dump rat.

She noticed Malachi's nose was bleeding when he pivoted and pointed the rifle at the old man still approaching, leveled and sighted down it.

"Stop right there," Malachi said. But the tone of his voice was all wrong. It wasn't an order. He was pleading with the man not to get any closer.

"It's hard when you see them things, ain't it — I know," the old man said and never stopped moving, slowly, inexorably toward where Malachi sheltered on the back side of the vandalized plexiglass. "Hard to know what's real and what ain't. Been there, done that, wore the tee shirt plum out, but I still use it as a dust cloth or to polish my boots."

Malachi said nothing, looked suddenly unsure, which

quickly downshifted into disoriented, confused. He was mad, frightened and … he grimaced and Charlie could actually see the reflexive movements of his diaphragm, as if waves of nausea were battering it. He was fighting it, but you could almost feel the explosive need to vomit … she could, anyway. Not half an hour ago she'd felt the same thing.

He somehow managed to keep his mouth resolutely shut, though, remained crouched on one knee up against the vandalized plexiglass of the bus shelter wall.

"Can you listen up to what I'm telling you?" the old man asked, and had moved to within twenty feet of Malachi. "You look here in my eyes, boy."

Malachi eyes were a frightened rabbit's, darting back and forth, clearly seeing something nobody else in that parking lot was looking at.

"Boy, you hear me!" There was authority in the old man's words. "I said … Look. At. Me." He said each of the words individually, like dropping stones one at a time into a still pond.

Malachi looked at him.

"I don't know exactly where you been, but you need to come on back now. Come on back here—" Malachi looked away and the old man grabbed his attention again — "Look at me!" — and held on. "Don't look out there at them other things because they ain't really there. Look at me. I'm real. I'm here. We in this world together right here, you and me, right now and nothing else you's seeing is."

Malachi's eyes shifted.

Focused.

Saw.

Then he looked around like he'd just opened his eyes after a bad dream and discovered he'd been sleepwalking, wasn't in his bedroom anymore, maybe wasn't even in his house. Recognition lit his features and he must have realized where he was. Or maybe where he *wasn't*. He carefully set the rifle down on the concrete, turned away from it and threw up.

Chapter Ten

Pete Rutherford was almost sure the young man havin' a flashback beside the bus shelter in front of the Dollar General Store was Viola Tackett's youngest — either Obadiah or Malachi. All them boys had Bible names and all he knew for sure was the oldest was Nebuchadnezzar. Seems like he'd heard in the barber shop that one of her boys come home wounded from some war or another he shouldn't have been fightin' in the first place.

When Pete came home from the South Pacific years ago, thin as a rail and covered in jungle rot, he'd thought he and his buddies would be the last American soldiers who'd ever have to pack up weapons and go fight somebody somewhere.

So he'd stayed in the military. And they sent him to Korea.

He got out then, way before they could pack him off to Vietnam.

And 'parently, this young man had been somewhere — he thought he'd heard Rwanda — and he was sure there was more wars lined up behind that one.

Pete was able to hang the right last name on the boy who was now dry heaving while Sam Sheridan held his head. You could deduce that much — them Tacketts and their black hair. But what was he doing in the Dollar General Store parking lot … well, technically in the bus shelter out front, at ten o'clock in the morning on a June Saturday, packing a .22 and clearly having an episode of PTSD? That wasn't as easy a thing to riddle out.

And the woman with the little girl wearing a head bandage like a princess crown looked like a Ryan, maybe Sylvia's youngest. Had she come with Sam? Had the Tackett boy come with Sam, too? They'd all three got here somehow, and wasn't but one car in the lot.

Didn't seem real likely they'd come together in that old Ford Taurus, but wasn't no other way they could have got here unless somebody dropped them off. What for? Wasn't like that shelter was a tour bus destination. Pete had just walked, of course, being as he was the lone resident of the unincorporated township known as the Middle of Nowhere, Kentucky. The little house he'd built with his bare hands … and the bare hands of lots of people he hired to come do the work he didn't know how to do … sat in the woods across County Road 278 East from the Dollar Store lot.

He was just out walking the stray mutt he'd named Dog after it adopted him, taking his obligatory morning "stroll" — like all them years he walked his route every day hadn't banked him enough miles so he'd never have to take another step. But Sam'd assigned him the walk as one of a half dozen daily tasks he had to perform "if you want to live 'til Christmas."

You ask Pete, him living 'til Christmas was about as likely as finding an honest politician. Though he was in remission and would stay that way for a right smart while long as he kept taking his treatments. Still … seventy-two years old and the big C. That was a bullet with his name on it. And it was time. He was ready to go. Just one last thing. He needed to say goodbye. So … not today, please Lord. Not today.

Oh, how he wished they hadn't told Jolene about it. Them medical people had asked him at some point for his next of kin and he'd put down Jo, his only daughter — didn't have no idea giving them her name meant they'd send her his medical reports! He put a stop to it soon's he found out, but he was just about sure she'd got the only one that mattered. What she might choose to do about that …

He shaded his eyes with his hand, squinting into the bright morning sunshine, and surveyed the whole empty area. Here was "the crossroads," the intersection of Route 17 that ran north/south and County Road 278, that ran east/west. Locals called County Road 278 East "Lexington Road" because it did *eventually* lead to the parkway and Lexington, and that's where most folks going down it were likely headed. The same road going west was called Danville Pike because Danville in Beaufort County was the next town of any size. He supposed the name switch happened at the crossroads. Route 17 was just "Seventeen."

The woods came all the way down to the road except for the expanse of parking lot where he now stood. There'd been some attempt at building a strip mall, he supposed, and seemed like it was E.J.'s daddy. The Dollar General Store had set up shop in a building of its own on the west end — with a drive-through on the side that had a machine you could use to vacuum out your car, an air pump to inflate your tires and a water hose.

The animal hospital was the only functioning business,

taking up two or three slots in the otherwise empty strip mall next to the Dollar General Store building.

When there had been a bus line running into Nower County, the bus company'd put up a right nice shelter — a long metal bench that sat beneath a wide roof held aloft by four-feet-wide panels of plexiglass on each end, with a lone streetlight hanging from a pole over it. Somebody'd been replacing that bulb because he could see the light from his front porch of a night. Lit up the sign "The Middle of Nowhere" right nice, he thought.

There was four stop signs, though he couldn't rightly recall ever seeing anybody actually come to a full dead stop at any one of them. You could see two hundred yards in both directions when you pulled up to the intersection and wasn't like you was gonna be blindsided if you gave it a quick left-right-left and drove on through. He still recalled being warned, as a young and exceedingly naive soldier in London right after the war, that cars in that fair city drove down the left side of the road and he would get his "arse run over by a bloody bus" if he didn't amend his customary left-right-left to right-left-right.

He watched a solitary pickup truck slow down as it passed through on Seventeen. Buford Haywood, who got his hair cut at the Barber Pole on Main Street in the Ridge same's Pete did. Though Pete still had a right smart head of hair for an old fart, Buford had so few lonely sprigs left in his chrome dome he'd said once he'd named every one of them.

Pete let his gaze follow Buford's truck, then swung it back toward the young used-to-be-soldier still heaving, leaned against the east wall of the shelter. That's why he saw it, the only reason he saw it. He just happened to be looking right at the end of the bench on the other side of the shelter when … suddenly somebody was sitting there.

So surprised he stopped breathing, Pete's walking stick clattered to the warm asphalt out of his suddenly numb fingers.

There was a person — it was Fish — sitting on the end of the bench.

He wasn't there ... wasn't *nobody* there. And then he was.

Not there ... there.

Holmes Fischer, in a rumpled jacket, pants that appeared to be wet on the bottom like he'd stepped in a puddle or a ditch, was clutching his floppy hat to his chest and staring blankly into space.

Pete let out a cry, he supposed. A grunt. A sound. Something. He made some kind of noise because the young woman with the little girl wearing the crown bandage turned to look at him and Sam lifted her head, too.

Then Sam squeaked a not-quite-a-scream her own self and her hand flew to her mouth.

She'd seen it, too. Well, maybe she hadn't been looking, as Pete had been, the exact instant Fish appeared on the bench. But she knew there hadn't been nobody there. Then she heard Pete's cry, looked up and somebody *was* there.

Out of nowhere.

Poof.

They both froze, staring in utter disbelief.

Fish sat stock still for a moment, seemed to settle into existence on the bench. Then he leaned over, choking, like he couldn't breathe.

Chapter Eleven

Charlie jumped back, startled, and gasped. She didn't scream, though. Sam had screamed, had *almost* screamed. The old guy — she was pretty sure it was Pete Rutherford — had cried out. So Charlie wasn't imagining it.

She saw it.

Sam saw it.

Pete Rutherford saw it.

She could tell by their reactions, which were as startled/stunned/disbelieving as hers.

There had been nobody in that bus shelter only seconds ago!

She replayed the video in her head.

She and Merrie had been there, on the other end of the bench, earlier this morning.

Malachi Tackett had been hunkered down beside the shelter dodging bullets nobody was firing a few minutes ago.

Pete Rutherford had come walking across the lot toward the shelter and Sam Sheridan had run to tend to Malachi.

But that was it! There had been *nobody else* there.

It wasn't like you could hide a thing like that. It was an *empty parking lot.* One car was parked in front of the Dollar General Store, either Sam's or whoever was working there.

There was not a soul in the empty bus shelter. Nobody sitting on the long bench in the shade of a roof supported by two plexiglass walls that bore a quarter of a century's worth of graffiti. No one was within sniffing range of the pile of cooling puke on the near end where she'd deposited the morning's toast and coffee.

There was nobody! Except ... yes, there was.

An old man in the weather-beaten clothing of a homeless person was there.

Charlie thought the man looked like an older version of Holmes Fischer, her senior English teacher in high school.

Whoever he was — Holmes Fischer or Elvis Presley or Bozo the Clown — he had *appeared out of nowhere.*

Just suddenly there.

And that, of course, wasn't possible.

But so was Charlie and Merrie being here.

Her knees suddenly felt like bags of water, unstable, like they might collapse and dump her on her butt on the ground.

She bent to one knee and put her arms around Merrie, ostensibly to comfort the child. In reality, it was a preemptive move to keep from falling. She was using Merrie to hold her upright so she couldn't faceplant in the parking lot.

How had she and Merrie gotten here?

How?

She had been driving down the winding road through the mountains, the windows down so the wind through the car would drown out the pitiful sound of Merrie's wailing, which had downshifted from a genuine reaction to actual pain to an emotional response to an opportunity to indulge in theatrics. Her little girl was a drama queen extraordinaire.

Then what?

Charlie remembered … shining black … static.

And the next thing she knew she was sitting on the opposite end of the bench where the homeless man seemed to be … choking, maybe.

He wasn't heaving, though, as she and Malachi had been, puking their collective guts out.

Not normal nausea. Violent, explosive nausea. Like a mini bomb in your belly, exploding the contents out into the world.

While she knelt frozen in place beside Merrie, Sam got to her feet, left Malachi on all fours, dry-heaving, and went to the man on the bench.

"Mr. Fischer … are you sick?"

It *was* Holmes Fischer!

He didn't respond, was clearly in some kind of physical distress but he wasn't vomiting.

She felt a shadow fall over her and looked up into the pale blue eyes of the old man who'd talked Malachi Tackett off the ledge. It was Pete Rutherford, alright, which meant he was definitely very old but he appeared to be in possession of all his faculties, which he had used skillfully on Malachi Tackett to bring him back to reality.

Reality. Right. Copy that. Reality. And realty was …?

"You got any idea what's happenin', ma'am?"

"Not a clue, but …" Her voice was trembly. She got carefully to her feet and looked Pete full in the eyes. Every marble appeared to be firmly in place.

"But I can tell you that … I don't know how *I* got here. How Merrie and I got here. I was driving down the road and then ..." She was reluctant to talk about the black-light thing. It was impossible to describe because it had been impossible. But that's what she had seen. All around her was light that was black, and she was afraid to discuss it for fear she'd start hearing the theme song to *The Twilight Zone*.

"Then ... go on."

"And then the next thing I knew I was sitting there." She pointed to the other end of the bench from the spot where Sam was trying to talk to the man who had hooked Charlie on fantasy — wizards and goblins and *The Lord of the Rings*. "And I was throwing up. So sick I ..."

"You didn't drive here?"

"You see a car?" She hadn't meant to snap. "No, I *was* driving ... and then I wasn't." She shook her head and felt a wave of vertigo wash over her. She must have wobbled on her feet because the old man reached out to steady her.

"Might be you need to go over there and sit down."

"And smell that puke? One whiff of that and I'll be off to the races again."

"So you're saying you don't know how—"

"I don't know how I got here and—" In for a penny, in for a pound. "And I'm wondering if I ... if I suddenly appeared on that bench like Holmes Fischer just did."

If she allowed herself to experience the true horror of that statement, it would have knocked her on her butt on the asphalt. Riiiiight, she just ... *appeared*. Wasn't there and then was. Happened all the time. Why just last week she'd been ice fishing in Antarctica, all bundled up in a parka, and the next thing she knew — badda boom, badda bing — she was in a bikini sipping a Mai Tai on a beach in Tahiti.

She recognized the wall of denial she was frantically building, refusing to see reality by making fun of it. But the

alternative was actually seeing reality, acknowledging it …
and right now Charlie McClintock could not force her
mind to countenance—

Sam screamed. This time, it was a full-bore, no-
squeaking shriek.

When Charlie turned toward her, Charlie saw a man in
uniform sitting on the bench. He hadn't been there even a
second ago. Had likely appeared so suddenly right beside
Sam that he had startled the scream out of her.

Charlie turned back to the old man with the clear blue
eyes and couldn't find the air to speak. From the look on
his face, he wouldn't have heard her if she had.

A whisper on a breath escaped her lips.

"What's going on here?"

Chapter Twelve

Sam was proud to discover that she wasn't totally freaking out, in the manner a situation like this clearly called for. She'd been too busy to freak, from the moment Abby Clayton had cried out, "Something's bad wrong here," until Holmes Fischer appeared — and he had *just appeared.* She could tell from the looks on the faces of the others that they'd seen the same thing she had.

First Charlie Ryan ... McClintock ... and her little girl. And then Malachi.

She came to a full stop then, just like all the drivers who came to those four signs at the crossroads intersection didn't.

Malachi. She'd heard he was home, but certainly didn't expect to see him for the first time in — how long? — crouched behind a bus shelter. As soon as he stopped fighting his imaginary battle, he was in the same condition she'd found Charlie — who had said she'd been driving down the road and the next thing she knew she was sitting in a bus shelter puking.

Sam had raced across the lot to Malachi, got down on

one knee beside him, but there was nothing she could do. She had only one other time seen someone retching as hard as he was. Charlie McClintock had been vomiting with the same ferocity, like in that movie where the alien burst out of the guy's stomach. It was like there was something inside Charlie and Malachi, trying to get out and they couldn't expel it fast enough.

There'd been nothing she could do for Charlie and there was nothing she could do for Malachi. She just held his head like she had done for Rusty so many times when he was little.

She was in that emotional space when Holmes Fischer appeared … just *appeared*. She saw him, she'd been looking right at him … well, right at where he wasn't and then suddenly was. Holmes Fischer, the county's token homeless drunk. Except he was technically not either. He had places he stayed. And when she thought about it, she realized he always looked disheveled, but he didn't smell bad, didn't look like somebody living in a cardboard box under a bridge. So he had somewhere he bathed, somewhere he kept clean clothes. But she didn't know where that might be.

Sam wasn't a doctor. Shoot, she wasn't even a paramedic. She was a licensed practical nurse who was paid to check in on people who were ill but not sick enough to be hospitalized, people who could stay home if somebody came by to keep an eye on them, take their blood pressure, make sure they were taking their meds properly and basically provide them contact with the outside world, which, in the end, was probably the best medicine she gave any of them.

But you didn't have to have a medical degree to see that Holmes Fischer was choking, and would choke to death in only a few minutes if somebody didn't do something.

She got up from Malachi's side, who likely didn't know she had left because he probably didn't know she'd ever been there, and ran to the bench in the shelter, kneeling in front of where Holmes Fischer was seated, gasping. No, not gasping. You had to have air to gasp and he seemed to have no air. Seemed to be desperately trying to breathe.

She had to stifle a little hysterical burst of laughter — Fish was like a fish out of water. But that was what he looked like, like a fish that'd been thrown out of the river onto the shore, his mouth open, gaping, trying to get in air.

"Mr. Fischer … are you sick?"

He didn't respond, but it was clear he couldn't. Clearly something was stuck in his throat and he couldn't breathe. She started to lean him over on his side on the bench but he fell that way before she touched him. She was able to grab hold of him and turn him so the momentum of his fall left him lying on his back. One good tug and she had scooted him to the end of the bench with his head dangling off it, opening up his trachea.

Sam wished she had something, anything to use to disengage whatever was causing the blockage in his throat, but there was nothing for it but to stick her fingers in his mouth …

And then Liam Montgomery suddenly appeared. Just appeared

The sight was shocking, surprising, but more than that it scared Martha Ann Sheridan in a way nothing else in her life ever had. This was really happening and her fear was too great to express with something as simple as a scream. You had to experience some kind of ground-zero, basic-humanity fear when you were confronted with a thing that was contrary to the laws of the universe. People didn't just show up — bang. Not just once. *Twice.* Two people had just … she wouldn't use the word "materialize" because that word brought to mind television shows and science fiction movies and this was everyday life in the Dollar General Store parking lot, for crying out loud.

But he is the greatest of fools, her father would have said, who continues to deny reality when it stands there in front of you, hot and stinking and demanding to be noticed. It was what it was.

Chapter Thirteen

Pete Rutherford had been breathing in and out at the good Lord's pleasure for going on seventy-three years. Not all that time was spent breathing the air of the Kentucky mountains, neither.

He wasn't the classic rube like so many of the people who lived in the hollows of Nower County were, so deep up in there sometimes you had to wonder if the sun actually made it there every day. There were people who had never left this county, who had never seen the outside world, what they called "out there on the flat," people who had never been to the big city, which they would define as Lexington, Kentucky. Fish had got out by virtue of the Second World War, enlisted the day after Pearl Harbor, not yet eighteen but lied about his age and they took him anyway. He was one of the soldiers the songs sang about, "How you gonna keep them down on the farm after they've seen Parieeee."

They'd put him on a train to California, then on a ship to the South Pacific. He had battled flies, jungle rot and Japanese soldiers, had made the close personal acquaintance of terror and loss during what were the formative years of a young man's life. It'd changed him. It'd changed all of them. Hard to surprise a man who'd watched his buddies get blown into so many pieces there wasn't enough left to ship home along with the dog tags.

But Pete Rutherford was surprised now!

In all his many adventures out there in the wide world and the blessedly quiet no-adventure life he had led in Nower County since then, he had never seen somebody just …

Just what?

Just appear.

There was *nobody* sitting on that bench. Pete would have sworn, would have taken a pistol in his hand, put it to his temple and announced to the universe that he'd pull the trigger if he was mistaken and there really *had been* somebody sitting there and he just didn't happen to notice.

That wasn't the way of it. And they was other witnesses besides Pete Rutherford to testify to the reality of what they seen that couldn't no way in the world be real but was.

Then Sam screamed *again*, a real scream, no holds barred and sitting on that bench down from where she was trying to clear out Holmes Fischer's throat so he could breathe was another somebody who just appeared — Deputy Sheriff Liam Montgomery.

He looked around, but wasn't no need. It wasn't like a police car had pulled into the parking lot and the deputy got out but Pete was tyin' his shoelaces and just didn't see it.

It was like the woman beside him suddenly came to life, like maybe she'd been froze there and suddenly thawed. At the sight of the deputy sheriff, she turned to Pete and asked, "Would you look after Merrie for a few minutes?" Didn't bother to wait for a reply, just looked down at the little girl and told her, "You're going to wait here for me. This nice man whose name is …?"

"Pete," he said.

"Pete is going to be right here beside you." The little girl tuned up to pitch a fit and then her mother said, "I'm going over there, just right there" — she pointed to the bus shelter — "and you can go with me if you want to but it's gross. People have been throwing up and—"

The little girl shook her head violently, the crown bandage flopping about, even took a step backward.

"Yukky!" she said.

"Then wait for me." She looked at Pete and placed the little girl's hand in his. Then she turned and was crossing the distance to the sheriff's deputy, who unlike the others was not vomiting. He was just sitting with his elbows on his knees and his head in his hands. And his nose was bleeding … gushing down his upper lip in a torrent.

"What's yore name?" Pete asked the little girl.

"Merrie."

"Oh, like Mary had a little lamb."

"No, like Merry Christmas, except with an 'ie' instead of a y," she said, clearly parroting words she'd been taught to say but didn't understand. She understood what she said next, though. "Why's everybody throwin' up?"

"Guess they ate bad beans," he said absently, watching Sam turn Fish back onto his side from his back where he lay taking big gulps of air. He started to sit up, Sam pushed him back down and he sat up anyway, shaking his head. Then his nose started to bleed. It was then that it occurred to Pete Rutherford that he didn't have to be totally useless. He didn't know more than the rudiments of first aid and couldn't move fast enough to do anybody any good in a crisis. But there was one thing here that needed doin' and he was just the man for the job.

"I need you to help me do something," he said to little Merrie, whose name was spelled strange, either to be pretentious or for some reason the little girl didn't understand and nobody else cared about.

He got the child to fetch the cane he'd dropped and then used it to accomplish a reasonably rapid hobble to the side of the Dollar General Store where the Clean Out Your Car machines were located. He picked up the water hose and turned it on and was rewarded several seconds later with a stream of water that actually had a decent amount of pressure. With Merrie's help, he uncoiled the hose and hobbled back toward the bus shelter, squirting the water onto the asphalt as he walked, washing away the stinking remains of the contents of several stomachs.

Malachi Tackett had gotten to his feet, though he still looked woozy. He stood, leaning against the piece of graffiti-ed plexiglass that formed one end of the shelter, holding his rifle, looking as thoroughly confused as everybody else. And it occurred to Pete then that there was, indeed, one thing more shocking than watching somebody appear out of nowhere. And that was *being* the person who done the appearing.

The woman, Merrie's mother, said she and the little girl had been driving down the road, though she hadn't filled in the blanks about why she'd decided to take an injured child for a drive or where she'd been going.

She'd been driving and then she was here. Wasn't no in-between.

Pete put his thumb over the end of the water hose to create more pressure and used the spray as a kind of broom to sweep the foul-smelling vomit off the asphalt and down into the roadside ditch.

If the others had had the same experience, then Malachi Tackett had been out squirrel hunting when the

… whateveritwas — a sudden desire to throw up in the bus shelter in front of the Dollar General Store? — had assaulted him. Fish, who was now sitting up with his head leaned back as Sam applied pressure to his nose to stop the bleeding, had been wherever he'd awakened after sleeping wherever he'd spent the night. Maybe he was drunk. Pete couldn't tell.

"I do it! I do it!" the little girl cried, begging to play with the water hose.

"Okay fine, you do it. Just squirt the water on the ground."

The child gleefully took the hose and began to squirt water every which way, but that worked because the parking lot was sloped toward the road and no matter where she squirted, the water would flow down that way washing away some of the yuk.

CHARLIE REACHED out to the young blond man in a brown Nower County Sheriff's Department uniform, sitting elbows on knees, cradling his head in his hands … as blood poured out his nose and dripped onto the asphalt.

When she touched his shoulder, he groaned.

"Are you hurt?" she asked him. He heard her, but it clearly took considerable effort on his part to lift his face up toward her and look at her. His eyes were bloodshot, the whites a veined angry red, like he'd just come off a week drunk, and there were dark circles under them. His face was chalky white.

"There's a needle" — the words rode a ragged whisper where every word seemed to deliver a painful blow — "in my head. A needle in my brain."

When he'd turned his face up toward her, the gush of

blood from his nose had changed direction, pouring down his lip to drip off his chin onto the front of his crisply ironed brown shirt. The name tag said he was Deputy Sheriff Liam Montgomery.

"It … *hurts*."

Charlie had no idea what to do or say. But she understood on an empathetical level that if the pain in his head carried with it anything like the force of the nausea that had hammered her, yeah … it hurt. It hurt *a lot*.

The young man carefully lowered his head back into his hands and held it there the way you'd hold a tray of Waterford crystal.

"Where …?" Fish began at the same moment Malachi Tackett asked, "What?"

Malachi had come around the side to the shelter and was standing, though wobbly, in front of the bench where Fish was sitting up, finally beginning to breathe normally, and the young sheriff's deputy was cradling his fragile skull in his hands.

Charlie looked at Sam, who was staring at Malachi with an unreadable look on her face. Then Sam's gaze shifted to Charlie and the two locked eyes. She could sense that Sam felt as she did, that somehow the two of them were "responsible" here, like the in-charge grownups at a party where all the teenagers were falling-down drunk. By virtue of being the first people on the scene of this … yeah, this *what?* And because the two of them — and the old man, who was helping Merrie squirt water out a hose to wash away the vomit — were the ones most in possession of their faculties.

Fish's eyes were clearing fast, though, but Malachi Tackett still had a dazed look and Charlie wondered if that might be his normal look, an expression that had nothing to do with suddenly finding himself beside the bus shelter at the crossroads and everything to do with why he thought an invading army was attacking him there.

"Anybody want to tell me what's going—?" That's as far as Fish got before Malachi Tackett sucked in a gasp, and then let the air out with a single incredulous word riding it.

"Mama?"

When Charlie and Sam followed his gaze, they saw a woman lying on her side in the grass beside the bus shelter. The woman was Viola Tackett.

Chapter Fourteen

When Malachi cried out to his mother, and Sam turned to see her lying in the grass beside the shelter, something inside Sam switched off. Or maybe switched on. She changed gears in some way then and seemed to go on some kind of autopilot.

Considerations of *how* and *why* and *what* became secondary to the reality that there were several people here in various conditions of physical distress. Physical distress was all she'd allow herself to call it because she didn't have any other names that didn't make her skin crawl.

She rushed to Viola Tackett and knelt beside her, with Malachi kneeling on the other side. He was calling out to her, had put his hands on her shoulders to lift her up, but Sam stopped him.

"We don't know what's wrong with her, Chai, and until we do, we shouldn't move her."

Chai. She hadn't meant to call him that. It'd just popped out but he was in such a state that he certainly didn't notice the word and by tomorrow morning wouldn't remember anybody'd said it.

"What's wrong with … where …?"

"I don't know and I don't know and I don't know. Until further notice, sprinkle those as needed at the end of every question about what's going on here."

As she spoke, she'd been taking Viola's pulse, which was thin, rapid and thready, but she didn't know what kind of rhythm would be native to a woman in her seventies who had led the kind of … shall we say "reckless" life Viola had led. Her breathing was shallow but regular. She lifted the woman's eyelids. Her pupils were not dilated and they were both the same size.

Turning toward Pete Rutherford, she called out, "Would you please go get Eli? I know he's there. I was just in his office—"

How long ago? Ten minutes? Half an hour? It couldn't possibly have been such a short period of time, in the world of minutes and seconds because in the world of life occurrences it was something like an epic. "Tell him I need his help."

Then she turned her attention back to Viola Tackett, who lay on her back in the grass unconscious. Not vomiting. No nose bleed. And until she woke up, they wouldn't know about the "needle in the brain" phenomena Liam was experiencing.

She groaned.

"Mama!" Malachi was holding her hand, patting it. It was such a tender gesture Sam wanted to look away, fearing she might tear up. She didn't. "Can you wake up and talk to me, Mama?"

Viola opened her eyes and immediately closed them again.

"Who burnt them beans?" she mumbled.

Sam and Malachi exchanged a look.

"What beans, Mama?"

"How many kinds of beans we got in the garden?" she snapped, but still didn't open her eyes. The strength in her voice was encouraging.

"Mrs. Tackett, this is Sam Sheridan. You remember me. I came out to the house when Neb got that spider bite and it got infected. Remember?"

"Onliest bite I remember was the goat got ahold of Obie's backside, tore the whole back out of his pants and got a good chunk of his butt with it."

Malachi smiled.

Clearly, the old woman was capable of lucid thought. She was confused and disoriented, but it didn't appear there was any serious—

Her eyes snapped open.

"Where's them boys?"

She made to sit up and Sam tried to restrain her but she shook Sam off like a pestering fly and sat upright. When she did, blood began to seep out of both ears and run down her neck. Looking around, her confusion quickly morphed into anger.

She spotted Malachi and dumped the anger on him.

"You want to tell me what you're doing here, and don't you lie to me, boy, or I'll snatch the hair off your head so quick your eyebrows'll be gone right along with it."

"Where is *here*, Mama?" he asked. Again, the kind, gentle tone.

"Why here—?" She looked around and closed her mouth. The anger drained off her face slower than it had flashed into place there and what came behind it was bewilderment.

Join the club.

She reached up to feel the wet on her neck and when she saw blood on her fingers, she cried, "What's goin' on? Where are … what are we doin'—?"

She made to get up and this time Malachi denied her.

"You sit right where you are until we're sure you ain't gonna fall on your face soon's you stand upright."

E.J. arrived right then, which wasn't the most auspicious moment in terms of dealing with a disoriented and confused Viola Tackett. His presence added another whole level of strangeness.

"You called the vet?" she cried, and her eyes flashed. "I … fell down and hit my head or whatever I done and you called the—?"

"You didn't fall down, Mama."

"Then you want to tell me what I'm doing on my butt in the dirt with blood drippin' out my ears?"

Instead of answering, Malachi simply sat down in the dirt beside her.

"I don't know what's going on." He looked at the people standing around. "I don't think anybody does."

"I do."

Everyone turned to look at Fish, who had gotten off the bench in the bus shelter and had come to stand beside it, completing the mini crowd around Viola that included Sam, Malachi, Charlie and her little girl, Pete Rutherford and E.J., who was accompanied by his receptionist, Raylynn Bennett, a beautiful black teenager whose crush on E.J. was so obvious it was embarrassing. There wasn't adoration in her startling gray eyes now, though, and they were the size of frisbees.

The only person who hadn't yet gotten up was Liam Montgomery. He still sat on the bench, holding his head in his hands, the blood from his nose slowed from a torrent to a drip.

"You *do* know what's going on?" Charlie asked Fish. "You want to tell the rest of us because we don't have a clue."

"There's a mirror across the road," he said, as if it were as ordinary a thing to say as "do you want to super-size those fries?" He looked from one to the other with a bemused expression. "You didn't see it?"

"And you did?" Viola said. "Are you saying that's how you got here — you stepped *through* a looking glass?"

At her words, all the amusement drained off Fish's face, replaced by something like shocked understanding. You could see the change.

"*Through the Looking Glass ...*" he whispered. He didn't sound drunk or even confused. He sounded scared. "And we must beware the *Jabberwock ...*"

The word raised the hairs on the back of Sam's neck. Charlie looked like she was about to start projectile vomiting again.

"... with jaws that bite and claws that catch," Malachi finished for him, in a voice hollow and unnatural.

"What in the world—?"

"It's nonsense, Mama." Malachi shook it off. "Through the Looking Glass is a book we studied in high school English, that's all. It doesn't mean anything."

And it didn't. Didn't mean a thing. But the little crowd was touched by the word and remembered it. It was like a nail in Sam's head where all the impressions of that morning caught and hung. Whatever it was that had happened to Charlie, Merrie, Malachi, Fish, Liam and Viola now had a name — the "Jabberwock."

Perhaps it was the sudden sound that hammered the Jabberwock nail so deep into their psyches. They all heard it for the first time at that instant, the sound of someone crying — *sobbing*.

With the unison of a chorus line, they all turned to look on the other side of the bus shelter. Someone was lying there, not far from where Malachi had crouched from unseen assassins. The spot was wet now, and water flowed out across it from the water hose that lay unattended on the asphalt after Merrie had lost interest in playing with it. Down the sloped parking lot to the shelter it ran, and around it on the downhill side washing away the remains of whatever had been deposited there, creating a small stream of rippling water.

A woman was lying on her side in the stream, sobbing. Sam got to her first, knelt and stopped, somehow reluctant then to touch her, curled up tight in a fetal position, her now wet hair covering her face.

She wasn't just crying. What she was doing might not even rightly be described as sobbing, either. It was an emotional state bigger than that, on the other side of that. She was wrenched by sobs, they wracked her body like seizures that shook her skinny frame from the top of her head to the bottom of her … she was missing a shoe.

The other shoe was a flip-flop, pink plastic, with a picture of—

No.

Sam backed up from the knowing of it like she'd spotted a scorpion on the ground, literally drew back, shaking her head.

The others now were looking at her.

"What …?" Charlie began.

And then Sam's body went rogue, refused to obey explicit orders. Her hands reached out, though she had strictly forbidden them to do so. Her fingers touched the wet blonde hair and gently moved it off the face that Sam absolutely could not bear to see.

It was Abby Clayton.

Abby Clayton had driven away from the Dollar General Store … how long ago? How long? Did nobody have a watch — *how long?* She grabbed Charlie's arm, who had knelt beside the girl on the other side, yanked it so hard she almost pulled Charlie off balance, had to get a look at her watch.

Ten-thirty.

Abby Clayton had driven out of the parking lot on her way to Lexington to collect her infant son about an hour ago. Stopping, say half an hour, at her sister Eva Joan's house in Frogtown.

Sam heard herself whisper out loud, "She probably didn't even make it across the county line."

Chapter Fifteen

It was going to happen today. It was, it was, it was, and Abby could barely hold onto herself for the knowing of it.

Cody was coming home.

Home.

And before he did, she was going to sit herself down in that armchair where they'd let her sit and hold him, feeding him them little bitty bottles of breast milk. That nurse with the big smile was going to place that precious baby in her arms and she was going to nurse him.

Then it'd be real.

Then she'd be a real mama.

Her baby son would be in a bed right there beside hers tonight, where she could see him and touch him and look after him every minute. The bed was a cardboard box she'd lined with blankets, with the new, soft blue one Shep's mama'd give her on the top. They didn't have no proper baby bed yet. They'd get one soon's they could, in Lexington, in one of them yard sales in some fancy neighborhood. They'd get somethin' real nice. But they was struggling now. With Shep taking off so many hours to look after her when she was pregnant, they didn't have hardly no money at all.

She looked down for about the hundredth time at the gasoline gauge on the old pickup truck. She had almost half a tank and that was more than enough to get to Lexington and back. But all she really cared about was getting *to* Lexington, about them putting that warm little bundle in her arms. After that she didn't care if they run out of gas and had to walk ten miles to get home. Long's she had Cody, her life was good as it could be.

The windows was rolled down cause it was a warm morning and the smell of cedar trees when she passed by a grove of them put her in mind of Christmas. She'd done bought the Baby's First Christmas ornament to put on the tree, seen it in the Dollar General Store last year when she just had found out she was pregnant. She'd gone in there to buy Shep some new socks because what he was wearing to work was so worn thin he was like to get a blister on his heel from his work boots rubbing.

But she come home with that ornament instead of the socks and when Shep seen it, he wasn't mad or nothing, said he was glad she done it and she'd spent the evening doing the best darning job she could on his socks so they'd hold up least till he got his next check at the end of the month.

She hadn't never in her whole life been as happy as she was when she found out she was pregnant, and that was a special kind of happiness she wouldn't never feel again so she treasured it up in her heart like the Bible said Mary done with what them wise men said to her about Jesus. It was special because it had all kind of emotions tangled up in it, and the biggest of the lot was relief. She *had* got pregnant. She *could* conceive.

She'd been so scared she couldn't, so scared that what

them drunk high school boys done to her after the ball game when she was in middle school had messed up something. She never told a soul about it, of course, didn't breathe a word. But she'd bled and bled and after that her periods was real irregular and they hurt. She was so sure she'd never get pregnant that when Shep started talking about getting married she'd said no, pretended like she didn't want to get married, didn't want to marry nobody, but she couldn't pull it off and he knew she was lying and she'd finally broke down and told him the truth, that she couldn't marry him cause she'd never be able to give him children. She never told him specific why not, and of course he didn't ask … talkin' about female things like that made men uncomfortable. And if she'd told him, if she'd said *who*, Shep would likely be in jail right now because he'd a took a baseball bat to all three of them and he was big enough to put a world of hurt on them boys.

Shep had said he didn't care 'bout kids — he was lying then, too, and they both knew it — said they'd be happy just the two of them and maybe someday they'd adopt kids. And so they'd got married and when she missed the first two periods it never occurred to her that it might be because she was pregnant. She just wasn't regular, that was all. But after the fourth one, she went to the doctor, worried something was wrong and when he told her what was "wrong" was she was three months along pregnant she had cried so hard she couldn't get her breath.

What'd happened after that, the pre-eclampsia and the staying in bed and Cody comin' early — that was probably the worst time of her whole seventeen years on earth. She woke up every morning so scared she was gonna lose the baby that her stomach was too tied in knots to eat. And she had to eat, had to force herself to swallow food like it was medicine.

When the baby was born early … so little. Didn't weigh but just over three pounds, so small Shep could have held him in the palm of his hand, Abby'd hung on every breath that child took, watched his little chest rise and fall with every one. She never left his side except to go to the bathroom. Not once, wouldn't let her mama or her sisters or Shep or nobody take her place beside that basinet. She knew it wasn't real, but she'd come to believe that her baby son was only breathin' because she was watching it happen, that it was her love kept his little heart beatin', and if she wasn't there, he would stop breathin' right then and die.

To this day, Abby couldn't have told you how long that part lasted. He was in the hospital for months, but if it was two or five, she didn't know. Time smeared together and all them days was like all the others of them, her sitting there, touching him when they'd let her, his little fist curled around her finger.

Willing him to breathe.

And prayin'!

She hadn't never been very religious, went to the Pentecostal church in the next holler over ever Sunday and believed the things the preacher said, but it hadn't seemed to apply to her life specifically until Cody was born.

She begged God not to let him die. Pleaded with God to keep his little heart beating. Promised all kind of things to God if he would let her little boy live and come home and grow up.

"God, if you'll let my Cody live, I will have that boy's bum on a pew every Sunday morning, Sunday night and Wednesday night for prayer meeting for his whole life."

"God, if you'll save my Cody, I will never raise my voice to that boy, won't never yell at him like them mamas

I seen in Walmart, screaming at their kids, cussing. I won't do nothing like that, God, I promise."

She'd got herself a little spiral notebook she kept in her pocket where she wrote down them things she'd promised God. She meant to keep them promises, every last one of them because God had *answered* her prayers and had *spared* her baby boy and in another couple of hours she'd be holding that child up next to her heart, nursing him, feeding him from her own body. She might not put him down for a month!

Glancing at the needle on the fuel gauge in the truck, she knew she was being silly, like maybe there'd come a big hole in the tank and all the gas'd drained out and her truck'd roll to a stop and leave her stranded. The Welcome to Nowhere County sign was just up ahead and she'd done the math like a hundred times, how many miles it was from there to Lexington and how many miles to the gal—

Suddenly the whole world burst into a million tiny pieces of sparkling black glass, flashing around her like a blizzard with black snowflakes, and there was a great roaring buzz in her head.

Chapter Sixteen

"The county line," repeated a voice from behind them and the group turned to look at Liam Montgomery who was standing just inside the bus shelter with one hand on the wall, leaning for support. His nose was no longer bleeding, but blood had soaked the front of his uniform and though he had done his best to wipe his upper lip and mouth on his shirt sleeve, blood was smeared across his chin. He spoke slowly and carefully, and Charlie instantly translated the body language. He still had a "needle in his head." She'd had migraines for years — not like some people she knew, totally debilitated by them, but she vividly remembered the incredible, not-like-anything-she'd-ever-felt-before pain of them. He was struggling to stand tall for all that and she admired him for that. "I was heading toward the county line," he said carefully. "I was chasing a speeder … with Pennsylvania plates … and I saw the sign—"

"Did you see me?" Fish asked, and Charlie could tell it hurt the deputy to turn his head to face him.

"No."

"Well, I saw you, threw up my hand and waved and then just kept walking."

"You were out there, on Barber's Mill Road?"

"I was."

"What were you doing—?"

"I don't give a rat fart what Fish was or wasn't doing on the side of the road when you passed him by," said Viola Tackett. She had not tried to rise, just sat in the dirt beside Malachi, who was looking considerably better. The color had returned to his face and his eyes looked like … he was here, with them, at least for the moment. "I want to know what *I'm* doing *here,* not what *he* was doing *there.*"

Several people spoke at once then, the general mumble expressing the same question. And the young blonde girl curled up in a ball in the puddle was still sobbing, wailing, hadn't diminished in intensity though she wasn't making as much noise because she was losing her voice.

"Why are you all … why'd you come …?" That was E.J. It'd probably have been a better idea to have left him out of it, but Sam had wanted somebody with some medical training to … yeah, to what?

"Ya'll telling me don't none of you know what you're doing here?" There was anger in Viola's customary brusque tone, but Charlie could tell that Malachi Tackett's mother was as uncertain, upset and confused as the rest of them.

"I think I was at the county line, too. I'd come down Sanders Lane from Route 17 to Lexington Road," she said. "I wasn't looking at the signs, but that's about where I must have been. Then … everything turned black."

Charlie'd had the most time to recover from … *the Jabberwock* … and her thinking had cleared enough to start putting some things together.

"And you heard static." That was the sheriff's deputy.

"Yeah, like when you can't get the radio station," Viola said.

"'Pears to me you all had the same experience in different places," said Pete Rutherford, and they turned to look at the old man who'd been hanging back from the crowd, mostly trying to corral Merrie, and had somehow interested her in picking dandelions out of the grass beside the shelter. "You was all on your way somewhere, ain't that right?" They all nodded. "And then you was suddenly here, sick, throwing up, noses bleeding. Like that."

"What in the Sam Hill could have … who brought you here?" E.J. wanted to know.

Nope, E.J. was definitely not helping. He hadn't been there to see the people "appear" like she and Sam and Pete had done and he was still operating under the common-sense assumption that somebody had brought all the people here, individually or at the same time, and he was trying to piece that together with—

"Clearly, you ain't listening, doc." Viola Tackett started to rise. Malachi reached to stop her and she slapped his hand away with enough force to deter another attempt. When she got to her feet, Charlie was surprised at how short she was. She'd heard of Viola Tackett since she was a little girl, but had only caught sight of her half a dozen times. And her memory was serving up to her from those occasions the image of a big, ugly, fat old woman with a voice sharp enough to cause internal bleeding and eyes that would pierce your soul. Her memory was conjuring up the physical from the psychological, and psychologically Viola Tackett was all those things. The reality of humanity standing before Charlie was a short, dumpy woman with a big bun of black hair at the back of her neck that made her look like an extra on some movie shot in Eastern Europe. But the eyes were like she remembered — bright and quick as a snake's.

"Didn't none of us come here a purpose." She looked to the others and nobody contradicted. "We's all on our way somewhere else and then … then we was here. Just here. If we all done what she done," she turned and gestured to the young woman sobbing on the ground, "we just appeared outta nowhere. I was lookin' and she just showed up, poof, didn't come walkin' up or get out of a car or drop out of a airplane with a parachute or nothin' like that. She just appeared."

Call a spade a spade.

Charlie had been dodging around, doing a mental dance, trying not to recognize that reality and Viola had just nailed it, straight up.

Viola surveyed the group as if they were the convicts on a road crew and she was the guard who'd caught them all leaning on their shovels.

"I want somebody here to tell me what's goin' on."

"I've told you, Mrs. Tackett, we all stepped through the looking glass," Fish said. And then more quietly, his voice tight, "where the Jabberwock lives."

"I don't mean some dad-gum story—"

"I'm not talking about a story," Fish said. "I'm talking about a literal looking glass. A mirror. There was one on the road. I saw it, saw myself approaching it. And when I touched it …"

"You's probably so drunk you's seeing double's all. A mirror in the road is … That's the craziest thing I ever—"

"It's no crazier than suddenly being here when none of us intended to be." Malachi was respectful to his mother, but she didn't cow him like she did the others. He looked around. "Anybody else see a mirror?"

When nobody said they had, Fish pointed out that he

was the only one among them who had not been driving when he saw the— he called it the "shimmer of the Jabberwock."

"If there'd been a mirror, the others might not have noticed it," Pete said. "From what I'm hearing, the only thing the whole lot of you's got in common is the county line. You's all crossing it — right?"

"So where's my truck?" Viola demanded. "I's driving it. It ain't here. So where's it at?"

"Must be parked out there somewhere beside my cruiser," said the deputy, who now had some color returning to his face and the pleat of pain planted between his eyebrows was softening.

Into the momentary silence that followed his words, a small, hoarse voice asked, "What's happenin'?"

It was the young blonde woman who'd been sobbing. She was sitting up now, with Sam steadying her shoulders, and her eyes looked like a baby owl's.

"I got to go get my Cody. How'd I get here?"

She sounded so pitiful, so lost and confused and frightened that it hammered home to the rest of them how bizarre and horrifying their situation was.

Charlie turned to E.J. "You got a truck? A van? Something we could all fit into?"

"Well, yeah, it's parked out back—"

"I don't know about the rest of you, but I want to take a trip out to the county line."

"Onliest thing I want is my truck," said the small voice of the blonde woman. "I gotta go get my baby."

Chapter Seventeen

Dr. Elijah Hamilton, D.V.M., didn't know whether to wind his watch or take third base. The day had begun as ordinary as any other, didn't go off the rails until Sam brought Charlie Ryan … no, it was McClintock now … into his office with her little girl who had a small gash in her forehead above her left eye.

E.J. didn't ask for specifics. Clearly, Sam was handling it, just needed some sterile supplies to clean the wound and had been nearby so she'd stopped at the clinic. There'd been a wreck or something. Some kind of accident. He had volunteered to take over the surgical duties, assuring Charlie that he could sew up the child's head so it wouldn't look like he'd been trying to construct a Frankenstein out of spare body parts in his garage.

He didn't think she would have agreed if she'd been in possession of all her faculties, but she was mildly disoriented and majorly confused, and while he tended to the child, she told Sam the most amazing story that began when the little girl had cut her head in the driveway of

Charlie's mother's house, had tripped over a tree limb that'd been deposited by last night's freak storm.

E.J.'d offered his condolences, when he'd had the chance, said he'd heard about Charlie's mother's death and he was sorry for her loss. Didn't say he'd been told the old woman had washed overboard in the ocean off the Florida coast and they never recovered the body — a story that seemed to be verified by the fact that Charlie had been at her mother's house and he'd heard nothing about a funeral or even a memorial service.

Not like there was a family plot or anything, though, the grave of her husband to lay her out beside. E.J. remembered when he'd first heard Charlie's father was a prisoner of war. They were in the third grade — he was in Mrs. Green's room, as was Sam, and Charlie was in Mrs. Baker's. There were only two third-grade classes, but there had been enough students among the county's dwindling population for three second-grade classes the year before and he'd been in the same room with Charlie that year. That was the year he'd fallen in love with her, and why his ears had perked up when he'd heard the teachers mention her name as he'd passed a group of them standing together in the hallway, talking.

"… *poor little thing, Charlene probably doesn't even remember her father,*" *Mrs. Baker says, with what E.J. recognizes as fake sympathy, like when his grandmother says, 'oh, bless her heart" about somebody when she's really glad some bad thing has happened to them.*

"*What must it be like to be Sylvia Ryan … with Bobby Joe just 'missing in action?'*" *said fifth-grade teacher Mrs. Pitt. All the kids were scared of her.*

"*Four years now,*" *said Mrs. Green.*

"And you know he's got to be a prisoner of war and they're just not saying," says Mrs. Pitt. "You know the North Vietnamese have him somewhere in some squalid prison, torturing him."

E.J. doesn't know what missing-in-action means, though he can guess. And he knows that he heard Walter Cronkite say on the news a couple of months ago that President Nixon was bringing American soldiers home from Vietnam. Now, he knows that Charlie not only doesn't have a father — he already knew that part, everybody did — but he's in prison somewhere or missing somewhere and nobody can find him. Both of those things sound so awful he wants to cry, but he's almost ten years old and almost-ten-year-old boys do not cry.

That's when he gets the idea to do something to make Charlie feel better. It's springtime and the tulips and roses are blooming in his neighbor's garden and he takes rose clippers and goes out right after sunrise and cuts a bunch of them for a bouquet. Charlie has a piano lesson every Saturday morning in the basement of the Methodist church and he waits behind Mr. Bohanan's garage for her to pass by on her way there, hiding so no one will ask him what he's doing with a handful of wilting roses and tulip stems — most of the tulip petals fell off right after he picked them.

He spots her, steps out and walks toward her as she comes down the sidewalk. When they're about to pass, he shoves the flowers out in front of him.

"These are for you." He had other stuff he intended to say, but now he can't think what it is.

"What for?"

"To make you feel better."

"Why? I'm not sick."

"No, but your father's lost and nobody can find him, or maybe he's in prison and—"

HE SURELY WOULD HAVE SAID other equally comforting things like, "they're probably torturing him," something sensitive like that, but he hadn't had the chance because she'd yanked the flowers out of his hands so forcefully one of the thorns on the roses stabbed into his thumb and it started to bleed.

"I don't want your stupid flowers!" She'd thrown the flowers on the sidewalk and actually stomped on them. But she didn't run away crying. She'd walked away, back straight, head up.

He'd loved her even more after that.

It'd been unrequited love all through elementary school and junior high school, but he'd gotten a girlfriend — Patty Sheedy — when he was a freshman and he'd forgotten about Charlie altogether.

Until today, he hadn't seen her since she'd walked across the gym floor to get her diploma the night they graduated. He'd left Nowhere County and gone to college, vet school, and endured a terribly volatile but blessedly brief marriage, before returning to set up practice here — because his father had built the strip mall and owned all the buildings and E.J. wouldn't have to pay rent. His clinic was one of, if not the *only* thriving business in a county that was dead, long dead, they just hadn't gotten around to having a funeral.

Will the last person leaving Nowhere County, Kentucky, please turn out the lights.

And when he saw Charlie today, he was stabbed with the awareness that maybe one of the worst mistakes of his life was giving up on a relationship with her all those years ago. She was even more beautiful now than she'd been then, her short dark hair shifting in silky strands in the breeze. When she'd first started telling that fantastic story to Sam about the black light and the static, he'd really thought she was joking.

She hadn't been joking. And now here he was with a van full of the oddest assortment of people he could possibly have assembled. On their way down Danville Pike to the county line, a little more than ten miles away. Since the Middle of Nowhere was … duh… in the middle of the county, it was an equal distance from the county line in all directions. At least as the crow flies. But the roads through the mountains meandered and switched back. The most direct route was the one they were taking, through the little town of Twig and out to the back side of the Welcome to Nowhere County sign to see if there was a mirror in the road there.

PETE WATCHED the van load of people pull out onto Route 17, his eyes following it until it had vanished around the bend. Then all the air kind of whooshed out of him, and he was tempted to go over and sit down on the bench in the shelter. But even though he'd washed away all the mess, there was a lingering odor. He couldn't smell it, hadn't smelled much of nothing in a right smart while, but he couldn't help imagining it and that didn't sit well with the current state of his stomach, the contents of which were black coffee and dry toast with no butter. Had to watch his cholesterol — you know, so he could live 'til Christmas.

He did need to sit down, though, so he opted to ease his old bones down on an upturned can that'd been left beside the Dollar Store when somebody cleaned out their truck. It'd likely held drywall mud. He reached down and scratched Dog under the chin and the old dog would have sat there between his knees getting his chin scratched until the Second Coming if Pete'd keep scratchin'. He told the dog to sit. It didn't. It lay down at his feet, though, which was just as good and he couldn't rightly expect the dog to obey commands when he hadn't never bothered to train him. But why should an old dog train another old dog to do new tricks? Seemed like a waste of time all around.

"You want to tell me now what's going on here?" he asked the dog, who looked up hopefully when he spoke, but didn't bother to get to its feet when it didn't appear a chin scratching was forthcoming. "'Cause I sure as Jackson don't know."

Sitting still like this, thinking, the events of the morning got even more bizarre in his head, and instead of puzzling out what might have happened, he found himself getting all tied in knots inside over the impossibility of *any* reasonable explanation.

He hadn't opted to go hauling butt out to the county line with the rest of them for a couple reasons. Oh, there was enough room in the van, but he couldn't have took Dog along. He'd only taken the dog riding in a vehicle once and he got car sick. He couldn't leave him tied up at the Dollar General Store, either, because he suspected the dog only submitted to the collar and lead to be polite, that the animal could escape either or both at will.

Mostly, he'd stayed because he had that uneasy feeling that whatever was happening here, it wasn't over. Best guess was, it was just startin'. And if that was the case, somebody else was likely to show up in that bus shelter out of nowhere and Pete had hung back here because it wouldn't be a good idea for somebody to show up without nobody around to see to them.

Oh, he couldn't minister to them like Sam could, and he wouldn't try — because he had neither the skill nor the inclination. He was grateful he couldn't smell the stink. Still, the retching sounds had forced him to clamp an iron grip on his own diaphragm so it wouldn't involuntarily join in the fun and games.

But he could be here, could use the water hose if he needed, could maybe make whoever it was understand that they wasn't crazy.

Chapter Eighteen

Nobody said anything. Not a word. As E.J. piloted the van down the winding mountain roads, it was as silent as a tomb inside. And after a little while, the silence was so solid it would have taken tremendous effort to break it. You'd have to hack into it with an ice pick and Sam didn't have the energy. Apparently, nobody else did either.

Charlie sat up front, riding shotgun with Merrie in her lap.

Sam sat in the seat behind them with Abby curled up against her, crying softly. She had never stopped crying. Just like Liam's nose had never quite quit bleeding. He was sitting on the other side of Abby and he kept swiping at the slow dribble down his lip with his shirt sleeve.

Chai and his mother and Fish sat behind them. Fish was humming some song with a haunting melody, not loud enough to be obnoxious and his voice was a deep melodious baritone so it wasn't unpleasant. But the melody eluded Sam and trying to place what the song was had begun to get on her nerves. Like there was so much going on in her mind and her emotions, just that one little extra thing—

"Put a sock in it," Viola told Fish and he stopped singing, quietly whispering the words to the Jabberwock poem instead. Its nonsense syllables became white noise that was somehow soothing.

"… brillig … gyre and gimble … vorpal sword went snicker-snack …"

Maybe the others were taking this time of communal solitude to order their thoughts, to examine sequentially what had happened in the past two hours, to begin formulating explanations or at the very least eliminating possibilities as they tried to puzzle it all out.

Not Sam. She just sat there, holding Abby against her like a lost child. Trying very hard not to think anything at all.

She'd spent a fairly pleasant minute or two floating on a barge down Denial River, imagining that she was going to wake up in her bed to the sound of Rusty banging around in the kitchen, ostensibly because he was going to fix his own breakfast but in reality trying to wake her up so she'd get up and do it for him. Saturday mornings were off days for them both. They always slept in as late as they could — her twelve-year-old had definitely inherited his mother's adoration of the human state of slumber. Theirs was a comfortable mother-son relationship where she didn't descend to the level of being his pal. He had plenty of friends and only one mother. But she always hung a little low on the branch of authority and he was such a good kid he'd never taken advantage of it. They were close, tight. If the lack of a father figure had affected him detrimentally, she couldn't see it.

But denial was hard to maintain with Abby sobbing

beside her and the weight of silence from the others heavy in the air.

Of course, this couldn't possibly be happening. But it was. Her coal miner father had raised all his children to be realists. It was what it was. Worse than useless, it was counterproductive to try to force reality into the shape of your own presuppositions about the way the world operated.

She coughed to cover up a bleat of inappropriate laughter. Maybe if she'd been one of them, one of the people who had suffered varying degrees of physical trauma, it would be easier to accept the unacceptable. But being merely a bystander to the carnage, no matter how closely she had observed impossible events occur, she still got stung every now and then with an urge to laugh at the absurdity of it.

People don't just appear out of nowhere.

Right. And you know that how?

Because it's never happened before.

And that's a valid argument — it's not happening now because it's never happened before?

What did that do to your interpretation of reality, your view of how the world operated and the functioning of the universe?

She realized that she was doing what she'd said she absolutely wasn't going to do — try to puzzle it out. But the human mind was like a dog with a bone when it came to conundrums. Somewhere in human hardwiring there existed the need to know — a *compulsion* to know — to understand, to figure out.

Where was Charlie's car?

Where was Liam's cruiser and Viola's truck?

Those were physical objects that objectively existed … somewhere. What was it her grandmother responded when she couldn't find what she was looking for: everything has to be somewhere. Simplistic as that sounded, it was a ground zero statement of the nature of the universe. Everything had to be somewhere. So where were their cars? Where was Abby's beat-up old truck? And the onesies she'd bought in the Dollar General Store. She's mumbled that they'd been on the front seat beside her. What happened to them? And the diapers she'd gotten at her sister's. And Charlie's purse? Did Malachi show up with his rifle because he'd had it in his hand when he hit the Jabberwock?

And was it just *people* who got channeled, transported, whatever-ed? If Viola'd taken her cat for a joyride, or Charlie'd brought along her pet monkey? Would those have remained with the missing vehicles? Or would they have shown up in the bus shelter in the Middle of Nowhere?

The Middle of Nowhere.

A chill went down Sam's spine. You get used to a word or a name, and no matter how silly it is in the beginning, if you use it often enough, eventually it sounds normal. You forget that the words themselves have meaning. What if … What if the reason the people had appeared in that particular spot — among all the ba-jillions of places they could have appeared — was because the spot was "the middle of nowhere." *Literally,* the middle of nowhere?

E.J. eased the van over onto the side of the road about fifty yards before the Welcome to Nowhere sign. Everyone sat where they were for a moment longer than was normal, perhaps a group reluctance to see what they were about to see and to know what they were about to know.

"Get the lead out," Viola said to Fish and Sam heard her slap him — on the shoulder or back … maybe on the butt. "I want you to show me this here mirror of yours."

Chapter Nineteen

Hayley Norman got into the car, reached up and adjusted the rearview mirror, then felt around on the bottom of the seat for the handle, pulled it and let the seat slide forward.

She shouldn't have done that!

She shouldn't have moved them.

But she couldn't drive the car if she couldn't reach the accelerator and the brake. She'd just have to remember to put them back the way they were. Hayley had made a list of all the things like that she had to remember but she hadn't thought to put the thing about the mirror and the seat position on the list.

It was a good, simple plan, but it hinged on using her mother's car for the day without her mother knowing she'd done it. Her mother would be at the nursing home with her grandmother in Carlisle from the time Daddy dropped her off on his way to work at the church until he picked her up after work. That was more than nine hours. Hayley had plenty of time to get to Lexington and then … they said it didn't take long, just a few minutes. Then she had to stay there for a while. But she had plenty of time. She just had to make sure her mother didn't know she'd driven the car. And she had that all figured out. Everything was on the list.

First — drive at least ten miles under the speed limit. No more than ten miles because she'd seen on television cop shows that it was suspicious if somebody was driving too slow and she couldn't get pulled over. Absolutely could *not* get pulled over.

Second. Watch out for other drivers because they're all idiots and she absolutely could *not* get into a fender bender. She would park a long way from the building. The hospital complex had a gigantic parking lot and she'd park way on the back row where there weren't any cars so she wouldn't get a ding on her door or scratch the paint somehow.

She would get back in plenty of time so the engine wouldn't be hot.

She would put only as much gas in the tank as she used — at that gas station in Lexington where nobody would know her. She couldn't do anything about the mileage, but she was certain her mother had no idea what the mileage was.

They'd told her that after the procedure she needed to have somebody there to drive her home and she had assured them, oh yes, she had somebody. Her boyfriend would be there. Right. Boyfriend. He'd be there. Riiiiiii-ight. But she'd had to tell them that or they wouldn't give her the appointment. Well, she'd just tell them something had come up and he couldn't come get her, convince them that she was fine, not woozy or groggy or anything so she could drive herself. She even had an extreme plan. If they wouldn't let her just walk out, she'd pretend to go to that bathroom on the second floor in the Women's Pavilion that had a door leading into it from two different hallways. She'd go in one, out the other and book it to her car. What were they going to do? Call the police? It wasn't against the law to get up and walk out of a hospital on your own after an outpatient procedure.

Procedure.

That's what it was. Hayley never used the A-word. Not since Sugar Bear had told her she had to get one, said the word in a cold, unemotional way like she'd only be getting her toenails clipped.

It was just a procedure.

She adjusted the side mirror and caught sight of her face and almost didn't recognize the girl with the haunted look in her eyes, the fear written on her face. Once she got through with today, Hayley Norman would not be afraid anymore. She'd just move on, go forward from here a better and wiser human being.

She patted her purse, made sure for the umpteenth billionth time that everything was there — the envelop with the money in it and her identification. The hospital required a picture ID. She hadn't had a driver's license for very long so the picture was recent.

And the money.

She let out a shaky breath. Didn't want to acknowledge that she was glad this was about to be over. It had stopped being exciting and fun to sneak around. He was no longer sexy and interesting. The older man image … it shifted in her mind. The definition was no longer "mature and confident, a *man*, not some teenage boy with acne." Now, older man meant he was old. He was her father's age and now he seemed like it. Particularly after she told him. His features had sagged, just *sagged*, and he had looked ancient.

She pulled the car out of the driveway and turned left on Hanover Street. Took the long way around to Lexington Road, then headed out. It wouldn't be long now. By this time tomorrow, this would all be just a bad—

The world suddenly turned black, shiny, sparkling black and Hayley's head filled with buzzing static.

EIGHT ADULTS and one little girl walked slowly down the roadside, watching the reflection of their approach in a mirage-like shimmer in the middle of the road.

Charlie was out front, holding Merrie's hand. She'd have made the child stay in the van but she was in no emotional shape to endure a tantrum. Yeah, okay, the little girl was spoiled.

"I see me," Merrie cried and if Charlie hadn't been holding tight to her hand she'd have raced ahead to the mirror.

"Well I'll be …" Viola didn't finish. Didn't need to. They were all staring gap-jawed at the apparition before them.

It wasn't really the mirror Fish had described, or the one Charlie had conjured up in her head based on his description. She thought he was claiming there was a literal mirror in the middle of the road, but that you couldn't see what was holding it there or the edges of it. That's not what she saw now.

It looked like a mirage, shimmering like it was undulating with heat waves in the desert. But it was clearer than a mirage. As they approached, their images were as defined as if they'd been looking into a clear pool. There was nothing "holding it" because it was a mirage, which didn't need duct tape to affix it. And you couldn't see the edges of it because there were no edges. It stretched across the road over the shoulder and down the embankment on the right into a puddle beside the road where a stand of cattails had grown up six feet tall.

The mirage crossed the road into the other lane, too, off the roadside there and into the trees that came down to a fence.

"Look in the background," Sam said. Charlie did, studied it for a moment and then she got it.

E.J. saw what she was referring to and leaned/fell backward onto the hood of the van.

The mirage reflected them clearly, but it reflected *nothing behind them.* The background was just a mirrored image of blue sky, with a thin veneer of white clouds.

E.J. turned, went back to the van, started the engine and pulled it up ten feet or so, stopped and got back out. It didn't matter. The van should have been parked in front of its mirror image, but it wasn't. Nothing was reflected in the mirage except the people standing in front of it.

Liam reached down and picked up a rock and tossed it at the mirage. It landed on the highway a few feet beyond the mirage and bounced.

"Looks like it's definitely just us," Fish said, "just people." He pointed up into the sky.

A flock of hundreds of starlings, a whirling kaleidoscopic of ever-changing patterns, was flying in an impossible wingtip-to-wingtip formation above them. The flock turned 180 degrees on a dime and executed a figure-eight movement that brought them swooping low over the nearby trees … and right into Beaufort County. The group stood silent for perhaps a minute, trying to absorb the implications as they watched the birds cavort back and forth across the invisible boundary.

"I don't understand any of this," cried Abby, hysteria close to the surface. "What is this thing? And where's my truck? I gotta go get my baby."

"I don't know what this is, ma'am," Liam said, trying to claim the role of responsibility a deputy sheriff should have had in the situation, "but I'm sure we'll figure it out—"

"Horse hockey," snapped Viola Tackett. "You figure something out when it ain't working like it's supposed to. You figure out what's wrong so's you can fix it. This here ain't something that ain't working right. This here is … it's a whole new something."

Abby straightened her back and turned on Charlie.

"What'd you do?"

Charlie was too surprised to speak.

"It was you done it. Had to be. You come from away-from-here, and soon's you showed up everything started goin' wrong. You messed up something," Abby said and gestured at the mirage. "Or brought somethin' with you."

Ahhhh, yes. Away-From-Here. The all-encompassing description of every place that wasn't Nowhere County. Any person from there was instantly suspect. If you couldn't trace your lineage back three, four generations, you absolutely were not to be trusted. Most of that kind of insular tribalism had faded away, but it was the historical canvas on which all their lives had been painted. And among the people who lived deep "back in the hollers," you didn't have to scratch very deep to find it.

"I was born here," Charlie said, and managed not to sound defensive. "Charlene *Ryan*. My mother was Sylvia Ryan — she taught ceramics classes." She paused for a beat before pressing resolutely on. "I'm a nowhere person same as you."

Everyone standing there had been born in Nowhere County.

Abby blew by her response, *mis*understanding spreading across her face.

"Yeah, it was *you*, alright. *You* done somethin'. Well, you got to *un*-do it. Whatever it was, you got to make it go away because I gotta go get my baby."

"This isn't Mrs. McClintock's fault," Liam told Abby and placed his hand on her shoulder. Abby slapped it away, her eyes narrowed in anger.

"Well, whatever you done ain't gonna stop *me!*" She spit the words at Charlie. "I ain't gonna stand here jawin'. I'm gonna go get my baby. I got to nurse him because he's hungry." She patted a small bulge in the hip pocket of her jeans. "I got promises to keep and long's I'm breathin' I ain't gonna break them. If I gotta walk, I'll walk. I'll hitch a ride. I stick my thumb out, somebody'll pick me up."

She took a couple of steps before Sam grabbed her arm.

"You can't, Abby. You're still shaking. You can barely stand up. You haven't recovered from … if you try to go through there …"

Sam looked like she'd lost the juice to complete the statement they all knew she was trying to make.

"You'll wind up in the bus shelter," said Malachi Tackett. "You won't step through that mirage to the other side like the rock did. You'll *appear* in the Middle of Nowhere." He paused. "Sick as a dog."

"That's crazy! It ain't right … something's not … I'm gonna go get my boy." She started back toward the mirage.

"Wait, Abby," Sam said. "Let me go first." And before anybody could stop her, Sam stepped forward and walked into her own reflection in the mirage.

And vanished.

Chapter Twenty

It was dark, but the dark was light and that didn't make sense but it was true. The dark was shining, illuminating the emptiness like a candle in a well. The sound was overwhelming, maddening, deafening, horrifying, felt like it was drilling into her ears, her nose, into any opening into her body and would explode out of it from the inside.

It was like static but not, more the one-note tone of a phone when you picked up the receiver — overlaid by a ragged edge of jittery sound.

Standing in the road, she had felt the warm spring sunshine on her face. Then the darkness.

Now her face was in shadow. Both the sunshine and the dark were gone and she was suddenly more desperately sick than she had ever been in her life. Her eyes flew open, she saw a smear of reality ... asphalt, someone standing in front of her ... Pete Rutherford and his dog ... and then she was vomiting.

She vomited more ferociously than she thought it was possible for the human body to eject stomach contents. It exploded out her mouth and her nose, tore through her throat with such force and violence it scraped the tissue raw.

The pain of the nausea in her guts was indescribable, a horror sensation that only emptying herself out would relieve, and she joined forces with her internal organs in an effort to throw up everything ... *everything*, couldn't get the vomit out fast enough, gasped and heaved and gasped and was aware of nothing but the sick feeling and the pressure to relieve it.

And the sound of someone beside her, a girl on the bench, sobbing, whimpering, "I can't see. Help me, I can't hear."

When the van marked Dr. Elijah Hamilton, DVM, pulled back into the parking lot twenty minutes later, Sam was still shaky, didn't trust herself to stand. Those who'd been with her at the county line piled out of the vehicle and Charlie rushed to her side, concern and relief fighting for purchase on her face.

"You're ... are you ...?"

Sam couldn't help noting who didn't approach or ask if she was alright, showed no concern at all. So let it be written, so let it be done.

Liam had Abby by the arm, holding her upright but restraining her, too, and she struggled weakly to get free.

"Lemme go. I ain't done nothing. Let me go get my baby."

"Case you ain't been payin' attention, missy, tryin' to go get your baby's only gonna land you right back here." Viola Tackett called them as she saw them. "And if I's to guess, I'd say you'll likely to be in worse shape than you was the first time you showed up."

Abby lost it. She leaned her head back, closed her eyes and screamed, *"What's happening?"*

"Yes, please ... what's happening? Where's my car?"

The question came from the girl who'd been sitting beside Sam. Hayley Norman, a morbidly obese teenager, fifteen or sixteen, the daughter of the Reverend Duncan Norman. When she'd arrived, she'd been blind and deaf, but that only lasted a couple of minutes, and she had been babbling about her car ever since she'd regained her sight and hearing.

The asphalt beneath Sam's shoes was wet where Pete Rutherford had rinsed it off, but the smell of vomit lingered.

"Try to leave the county and you wind up here … somehow," offered Liam. "Doesn't appear to matter where you cross the county line." They had obviously talked in the van about what had happened to them, compared notes, still he looked around for confirmation he didn't need. It was obvious the people standing around him had not all been in the same place when … whatever happened happened. The only common thread that sewed their circumstances together was the county line.

There'd obviously been discussion of the why on the way back, too. There were no limits to the possibilities because it was impossible. Sam figured it was most likely some absurdly rare meteorological phenomena related to the freak storm that had blown through the county last night.

"This is crazy," Abby shrieked. "I gotta *gooo*. My Cody's waiting for me to come get him." She turned to Charlie, not angry anymore, pleading. "Make it go away, this Jabberwock. I'm begging you. Make it go away, *please*."

"Where's my car?" Hayley asked, still disoriented. "My mother doesn't know I took it. I was gonna be back before …"

"They's gonna be other people here," Pete Rutherford said. "If … whatever this is … if this Jabberwock thing keeps happening, people are going to keep showing up here. I'd say it ain't gonna be long before they's a considerable number of sick, hurtin' people in this parking lot."

"What's the population of Nower County?" Charlie asked. Nobody answered. She looked around. *You mean nobody knows how many people live here?*"

"I suspect it'd be more accurate to say nobody *cares*," Viola said.

"It's not as simple as it sounds." Sam tried to explain. "Nower doesn't have county government, no incorporated towns, so our numbers get lumped in with the surrounding counties in statistics. The circuit judge has jurisdiction in four counties and Nower's *one* of them. I work for the state health department in Nower, Beaufort and Drayton Counties. Our Congressional District is six counties ... you see?"

"A guess, then," Charlie said. "An estimate."

"Two thousand people," E.J. said.

"It's more than *that*," Pete said. "More like three thousand ... maybe thirty-five hundred."

"Thirty-five hundred people in Nower County!" Viola scoffed. "What rocks is all them people hidin' under? If they's even a thousand people live here I'm my own grandpa."

"The tax rolls aren't accurate because so many people don't pay taxes," Liam said. "But last time I looked, there was four tho—"

"Don't nobody but me care what's happenin'?" Abby cried, looking from one to the other. "It don't matter how many of us they is, can't none of us leave and" — she turned on Charlie — "it's *her* fault. Somebody make her fix it!"

"Pete's right," Liam said, ignoring the outburst and trying to circle the conversation back to Pete's concern. Liam was trying to sound official, hard to do with the front of his shirt stiff from dried blood and a dribble still edging down his lip from his left nostril. "We need to report this."

"To …?" Viola Tackett asked.

"The State Police Post in—"

"I don't think you can call out of the county," E.J. said. "I called Jeb Pruitt in Twig early this morning and got through fine. But then I tried to call Lexington, three or four different numbers — where we order antibiotics, places like that, and got nothing, not even a busy signal."

"Local people, then. We need to warn—"

"How?" Pete Rutherford asked. There was no radio station in Nowhere County.

"We need to tell people not to—"

"Not to what?" Viola said. "Not to try to leave the county?" She bleated a chuckle. "Run that up the flagpole and see how many folks you can get to salute." She shook her finger at an imaginary somebody, "'Ya'll need to stay home now, because if you don't, you'll wind up puking your guts out at the Dollar General Store.' Who you think's gonna believe a thing like that?"

"I still think we have to try," Sam said, speaking for the first time, her normally deep voice an octave lower because she was hoarse. "A phone tree. We could spread the word that way. Edith Wilkerson's got a big prayer circle and we could …" Even as she said it, she realized it would be sticking a finger in the dike. "It's just that after going through …" She actually shuddered. "There are people in this county — old, sick — who might not *survive* the Jabberwock."

"I need to call in," Liam said. The sheriff was likely out of the county, fishing. He went fishing every weekend at Lake Cumberland. But maybe the other deputies were at home. Liam's radio was in his cruiser, so he started toward the Dollar Store. "I'll borrow a phone."

"Use my office," E.J. said. "There are two lines. Anybody else who wants to call …?"

Viola turned to Malachi. "Call Neb. Tell him to come get us."

Sam knew what she meant was to call the Martins, who lived at the bottom of the ridge, give them a message. The Tacketts didn't have a telephone.

Abby rushed to Sam and grabbed her hands.

"Please, you got to help me. I got to get up Lexington. My Cody's waitin' for me. Will you take me?" Abby gestured toward Sam's car, the only one parked in front of the store, though there were now a dozen people in the parking lot. "You still got a car. You could take me. I'll pay you." She looked around, disoriented, only just now missing the purse she must have left in her truck. "I ain't got no money now, but I'm good for it. You know I am. Just … *please* …" The desperation in her voice was heart-breaking. *"Please help me."*

"Abby, we don't know what's going on or how long it will last, but we *do* know that right now, you can't cross the county line or you'll just end up here, sick." The girl was devastated and Sam fought for something to say that would make her feel better. "Nobody knows what it is, why it is. It just appeared and I'm sure it's going to disappear the same way — poof, not there anymore. Then life can go right back to normal."

"You think it's just gonna go away?"

How would Sam know? In truth, Sam did *not* think it was going to go away, though she had absolutely nothing to base that belief on, no empirical data to support it. Of course, she couldn't tell poor Abby Clayton that. "Sure I do. We'll wake up tomorrow morning and it'll—"

"Tomorrow!" Abby couldn't have sounded more horri-fied if Sam had suggested she build an altar to Satan right

there in the parking lot and sacrifice her baby son on it. "I can't wait until *tomorrow* to get my baby!"

She looked into Abby's faded-blue eyes, focused on capturing her attention.

"Look at me Abby. Listen. I *will* help you. I *promise* I will. But right now helping you means not letting you go running off into the Jabberwock—"

"The Jabberwock. The Jabberwock. Stop calling it that!"

"—and making yourself sick. Are you listening to me? Do you understand what I'm saying to you?"

"Onliest thing I understand is I ain't there and my baby needs me." She looked down at the front of her shirt where a wet spot had appeared. "*See there!* See what I mean. I been pumping so there'd be extra for when I come home. But they done used that up by now and it's time to feed him. I'm supposed to be there — *right now!* — nursing my baby."

"I will take you to Lexington myself, okay? I will drive you to the hospital and go in with you and help you gather up your baby's things. Just as soon as it's possible to leave. But it's not possible right now."

Abby said nothing, just looked daggers at Charlie. Then she shook her head and made some kind of sound, like a baby rabbit run over by a hay baler. She sat down, right there in the middle of the parking lot, put her head in her hands and started to cry.

Holmes Fischer was standing nearby, looking worn and desperately in need of a drink. He looked at Abby and announced to everybody and nobody:

"Anybody given any thought to the other side — out there beyond the Jabberwock? The people who are expecting us." Abby looked up when he said that. "When Abby here doesn't show up at the hospital. When Hayley doesn't show up at" — he turned to the teenager who'd just regained her sight — "where was it you said you were going?"

The girl looked like he'd kicked her in the belly with a pointed-toe cowboy boot.

"I wasn't going *nowhere!* I just borrowed my mother's car to … go for a ride, that's all."

Fish blew her off.

"Well, whatever. The point is that somebody out there is bound to start wondering what happened to us." He smiled down at Abby. "And come looking for us."

The hope that bloomed on Abby Clayton's face was as bright as her smile had been a hundred years ago when she'd been buying a package of onesies in the Dollar General Store.

"Ya think? Ya think somebody'll come?"

Sam quickly put a smile on her own face that fit there like a stick-on name tag. Somewhere deep inside, the Essential Sam didn't believe for a minute the Jabberwock could be beaten that easily.

Chapter Twenty-One

In a reasonable world — which this had ceased to be the moment they'd all fallen off into black light — Sheriff's Deputy Liam Montgomery would have stepped in and organized all that came after the trip to the county line. He was, after all, a sworn-in law enforcement officer. But a uniform did not a police officer make. Liam was still mildly disoriented. His nose had never completely stopped bleeding, and it quickly became clear to Charlie that he didn't have a whole lot of experience — as a police officer or anything else.

Liam had called in to the sheriff's department to confirm that Sheriff Mason had, indeed, gone fishing in Lake Cumberland yesterday, which left Liam and Senior Deputy Skeet Phillips on the hook for policing. Phillips was nowhere to be found. The sheriff's department operated out of a little office in the Ridge, the only one of the handful of communities in the county that was formally incorporated into a town, though it had been unincorporated at some time in the past and Charlie didn't know when or why. Maybe there hadn't been a why. Maybe it had just been a process of decay, like a shoelace gradually coming untied so that it gets looser and looser until the shoe finally comes off altogether. It wasn't likely there'd been an official un-incorporating ceremony, complete with a bottle of champagne to shatter over the bow of the not-a-legal-town-anymore to christen it. It was more likely it just happened when nobody was looking and by the time they did notice it didn't matter anymore because they didn't care.

Charlie had taken Merrie on a little tour of the county when she'd first arrived early yesterday morning. An excuse for nostalgia. Coming here for the last time seemed to mandate a survey of her past, her "heritage." The old man who owned the strawberry patch where she used to go with her mother to pick baskets full of berries the size of ping-pong balls had come back to Nower County to live after the First World War and her mother had asked him why he'd returned. He'd said the one thing in life they can't take away from you is where you're from.

"You can lose your house, you can lose your family, you can lose a bet, you can lose your job, or your driver's license or your mind or your will to live or the card that tells you the date of your next dentist's appointment," he'd said, "but you can't never lose where you're from. That's yours for permanent, for always."

But as time went by, Charlie had come to think of where she was from as less a thing she couldn't lose and more something she couldn't get rid of. Like gum on her shoe, the little nowhere place in the Kentucky mountains would always stick to her. It had in some ways defined her, she knew, though she couldn't have articulated how that was. After she left, it became merely an empty spot in her mind where she never went, the reality of it a "nowhere" populated by people trapped by circumstances. Charlie didn't know anybody who'd actually moved to Nower County on purpose.

No, that wasn't true. There had been the Amish family named — what else? — Yoder who had stayed on after they'd built her mother's kiln.

Sylvia Ryan had transformed the two-car garage on their shallow three-acre lot at the base of the mountain into an art studio when Charlie was in elementary school, and no car ever saw the inside of it again. One whole side was nothing but shelves, built at right angles to the wall with walk space between; they were the residence of all manner of pots, bowls, vases, cups, ashtrays -- just about anything you could make out of clay — that her mother sold in shops all over the eastern part of Kentucky, West Virginia and Tennessee. The other side of the garage was home to a potter's wheel and to long tables with benches where she conducted classes to teach others how to make an ashtray. Taking a "ceramics" class from Mrs. Ryan — particularly since there was no charge for the class and supplies were furnished — was enough of a curiosity that probably half the women in the county had eventually shown up to take advantage of it.

Most of the "students" had no idea that making a pot or a bowl or an ashtray required so many steps and that the end products had to be fired in her mother's kiln.

Charlie remembered construction of the kiln because the outside structure that sat in the back yard beside the garage door was built by a crew of Amish stone masons from Pennsylvania and they were an oddity her friends actually came to her house to see.

Their haircuts were ridiculous, the buttons on their shirts and pants didn't match and most of them were in dire need of serious dental work.

The kiln they built was a six-by-six-by-six-foot marvel

with stone walls a foot thick and a door that sealed airtight. She and her friends had watched from the window of her room as the Amish men cut the stone pieces from larger pieces of stone and fit them together so tight you couldn't slide a piece of paper between them — "as tight as an Egyptian pyramid," or so her mother claimed.

Her mother'd paid to have a lock installed on the door above the handle and she kept it locked whenever she wasn't using it, didn't want some kid to wander in and get trapped there.

A company from Louisville had come down and installed the guts of the kiln that fit inside the stone walls. A control panel just inside the garage was equipped with all manner of dials, knobs and gizmos to set the temperature. The kiln had its own designated gas line from the big butane tank that used to sit in the backyard.

A couple of months after the kiln was complete, Charlie was stunned to see a horse and buggy clip-clopping down Barber's Mill Road. Her mother told her the Yoders had liked Nower County so much, they'd moved to a little farm down the road. Charlie didn't know if there were still Yoders living in the county, or if they, too, had drifted away.

Nower County was a good-sized place in terms of landmass and geography. But it was in the mountains and the majority of its acreage was uninhabitable by virtue of it being — duh — on the side of a mountain. Farms like the Yoders' were sandwiched into narrow hollows.

A handful of small communities dotted the landscape.

One was called Killarney in the southeastern part of the county, where the mountains were steep, the hollows deep and the residents standoffish and clannish. The Tackett family had lived in those mountains for generations.

One of the communities was called simply Twig. It was a collection of houses, a Pentecostal church building and its accompanying cemetery. The building had been vacant when Charlie left and it still was, so dilapidated now it looked ready to collapse. But the cemetery appeared to be a growing concern. Clearly, there were three or four times as many dead people in Twig as living.

Wiley was a community in the northwestern part of the county near the Rolling Fork River, which snaked along, back and forth between Nower and Beaufort Counties. The Wiley Bridge was an authentic covered bridge that spanned it in Nower County, a historic structure that was ruled unsafe for school buses when Charlie was still in grade school. There was no way to get the kids from the northern part of the county to school in Persimmon Ridge without crossing the river. So the bus stopped, the kids got off, the bus crossed the bridge, the kids crossed on foot behind it and got back on the bus.

Ten miles south of Wiley was the community of Persimmon Ridge, which was neither on a ridge nor boasted the presence of a single persimmon tree. It had been for a time a real, legally incorporated town. Known only as "the Ridge," it had had a post office, a small courthouse that housed the property valuation administrator's office, the county clerk, the office for the circuit judges who rotated through a four-county circuit, a big high-ceiling courtroom that took up most of the second floor and the sheriff's department that served the whole county with a handful of deputies and half a dozen cruisers.

The Ridge had even had a "jail," a small building not a whole lot larger than a two-seater outhouse with bars on the lone window where you could lock somebody up until the state police had time to pick them up and transport them to Carlisle. The Ridge had a small hospital/nursing

home, two resident doctors and a chiropractor, three
dentists — an old man who had brought in the younger
men so he could retire — a volunteer fire department,
three schools — elementary, middle and high school — a
Masonic Lodge and a funeral home.

Main Street in the Ridge had boasted a couple of
banks, real estate offices, attorney's offices, a restaurant or
two, furniture stores and clothing stores.

Then the coal mines, which had provided steady
employment to a huge percentage of the working men in
the county, closed. Three factories in neighboring Craw-
ford County to the east — an underwear factory, a casket
factory and a factory that built cupolas and church
steeples, called the Steeple People, shut down, and put the
Nower County residents who commuted there every day
out of work. An industrial complex in Lexington had
employed a surprising number of Nower County residents.
When it downsized, they all lost their jobs.

Then the parkway that would have brought the world
back to the county was built in Beaufort County instead.

There were probably dozens of other reasons —
Charlie was no sociologist — why the town and the county
had died. They just had. Victims of the domino effect of
economic circumstances. The jobless moved away, looking
for employment, the young left after school, never to
return. With fewer and fewer customers, the small businesses closed. The dwindling tax base and smaller number
of students forced the schools to close. Not enough patients
for the doctors, the dentists and the hospital. The post
office was shut down. One thing after another had reduced
the Ridge to … not a ghost town, that would have been
better, Charlie thought, more scenic. Everything gone,
doors on broken hinges, shutters blowing in the wind, a
tombstone on the site of a dead community. What had

actually happened to the Ridge and to the rest of the county in other individual ways, was they *hung on. Almost* everything closed ... but a store or two here and there managed to make it. A beauty parlor. A pool hall. No official community services, but the sheriff's department still employed an elected sheriff and a couple of deputies ... and Charlie had no idea how they were paid or where the department got the funding for the upkeep of an office or vehicles. There were fire trucks and perhaps volunteers to man them. Charlie'd seen the trucks at the fire station when she drove by. But on the whole, starting long before Charlie graduated from high school and accelerating in the years afterward, Nower County *literally* became Nowhere County, its people nowhere people. And with the passage of years, the county slowly sank below the horizon of the consciousness of the outside world. Like it didn't exist.

Chapter Twenty-Two

What followed her return in E.J.'s van from the mirage on the county line to the parking lot of the Dollar General Store in the Middle of Nowhere was the longest day of Charlie McClintock's life. Every minute seemed to take an hour and as the hours stacked up one on top of the other like a pile of cordwood, the world got stranger and more unmanageable.

By virtue of — Charlie didn't know what; nature hates a vacuum, maybe? — she and Sam Sheridan had fallen into the role of "in charge" at this disaster scene, which was what it rapidly became. It was as if a tsunami had crashed down on the county and the Dollar General Store parking lot was where the survivors had washed up on shore — in various levels of incapacitation.

Oh, she and Sam weren't forced to take the job. They could have bailed, left, gone home — shoot, Charlie had tickets on a plane back to Chicago tomorrow night and she'd barely started going through her mother's things. But you didn't just turn your back and walk away from a catastrophe and leave the victims lying there sick and bleeding.

You helped. You did whatever you could. That was the price of admission to the human race.

Charlie loved football — had loved it even *before* she'd married Stuart. She understood the phrase "calling an audible." That was when the quarterback's play wasn't working and he called out a new one on the fly. She and Sam hadn't had much of a play designed in the first place — a hasty "I'll take care of the new arrivals" from Sam and an "I'll see to the walking wounded" from Charlie. And that play quickly disintegrated into all the players calling audibles all the time. Controlled chaos. *Controlled* most of the time. Some of the time.

The moniker Fish had hung on the phenomenon became more fitting by the hour. The people of Nowhere County had somehow been pulled through a mirror into a whole new world where the usual principles of the functioning of the universe flat out did not apply anymore. And the foreignness of it all — each new person who looked at them with confused eyes and asked "Where am I? How did I get *here?*" couldn't have been any less frightening than wandering through Wonderland, fearing an attack any minute by a monstrous dragon called the Jabberwock … and you'd left your magical "vorpal sword" in your other pants.

When Malachi's brother Neb — short for Nebuchadnezzar, which it was rumored he never did learn how to spell — arrived to pick up Malachi and his mother, Malachi refused to leave.

"They need help here," he said, to which his mother replied, "This ain't none of your concern, boy." To which he replied, "Then whose concern is it?"

Charlie didn't know what Malachi's rank had been in the military — didn't even know which branch he'd served in — but he was as good at giving orders as he was at taking them. He was good at organizing, too, and devised systems and some semblance of organization as they assembled the growing number of volunteer helpers into teams to assist Sam and Charlie in caring for the fast-growing number of Jabberwock victims, getting them back on their feet and into the shade of the roof overhang on the line of empty strip mall businesses. When they were finally able to stand and think, they used E.J.'s phones to call someone to come get them or found a ride home with somebody already there.

A warning would have done no good, of course, but Sam *had* been right in suggesting they could get the word out on the phone, neighbors calling neighbors. It was testimony to the hardy nature of the county's bird population that the ones perched on phone lines didn't get fried by the friction of all the calls suddenly going through the wires.

Word of the phenomenon spread like a grass fire. When people heard, they did one of three things. They blew it off and went on with whatever they'd been doing. They raced out to their nearest juncture with the county line to prove that it was just some made-up story that didn't have no truth at all in it. Or they showed up as gawkers and looky-loos at the Middle of Nowhere crossroads, wanting to see the "popping into existence" part with their very own eyes.

Those were the ones that got under Charlie's skin. Rubber-neckers. Many — not all of them, but a lot — were the kind of people who stood below some poor soul out on a ledge and yelled, "Jump!" They had come to see the show and when she looked at their faces she could find not a speck of compassion for their neighbors. They'd spent their lives rubbing elbows with the sufferers, but in Nower County there appeared to be a sizable chunk of humanity who knew little more about their neighbors than their names — and whatever piece of juicy gossip happened to be attached to their family history.

There was an onslaught of teenage boys for a while who'd wanted to "take a ride on the Jabberwock" as soon as they heard. Since the phenomenon was clearly a fluke, some freak of nature that wouldn't last long, the teenagers were determined not to miss the excitement while it lasted. A group of half a dozen of them had raced out to the county line somewhere and dispatched the driver's girl-friend to the Middle of Nowhere to pick them up so they could all go out and ride in again.

When she arrived, her boyfriend's buddies were sick as dogs. Vomiting. Nose bleeds. And all the shine went completely off the pumpkin for the poor girl when she found her *Stud*ley Do-Right boyfriend suffering from bloody diarrhea. When word about *that* got out, the number of teenage "incoming" fell off markedly, though the number of gawkers in the Middle of Nowhere continued to grow at a steady rate, as folks decided it was safer to come see what had happened to *other* people before subjecting themselves to the effects of the weird, shimmering mirage that encircled the whole county.

At some point, Malachi had started "requisitioning" clean clothing and other supplies from the Dollar General Store. The owner, Howie Witherspoon, was nowhere to be found. The teenage checker who had not one time ventured out into the parking lot put up little resistance, particularly after Sam handed her a credit card and said she'd pay for whatever they used. Charlie knew Sam didn't have that kind of money to throw away. Charlie did, of course, but her credit cards were in her purse in the airport rental car ... wherever that was. Eventually, the checker just walked out, left the door open. Maybe she locked up the register ... or not.

Pete Rutherford put himself in charge of what he called the Yuk Squad.

"I don't get no credit for being self-sacrificing," he said. "I got almost no sense of smell no more. It was a shame at first not to be able to smell bacon fryin' or coffee brewin' or the air after a spring rain. Went and bought myself some baby powder, dusted it all over my hands, put them over my nose. Nothing. I liked to a cried." He looked out over the parking lot. "But it's definitely an advantage right now."

Sam was soon overwhelmed with trying to care for all the desperately sick people. Their maladies ranged from projectile vomiting, nosebleeds, bleeding ears, confusion, disorientation, temporary loss of hearing and/or vision to migraine headaches and bloody diarrhea. The symptoms and their severity differed dramatically from person to person — for no apparent reason, with no pattern they could discern.

Two healthy teenage boys and a farmer named Judd Phillips, who was as strong as — and built like — a bull, had been totally incapacitated for more than two hours, too sick with vomiting and headaches to move. But five-year-old Timmy Bessinger, whose mother was taking him to a dentist appointment, had gotten off with mild disorientation and a kind of blank stare that lasted for about half an hour — much like Merrie's.

Seventy-nine-year-old Grace Tibbits showed up with her son Reece, who was taking her to Carlisle for her twice-a-week appointment for dialysis.

It hit Charlie then, and she saw it sink in with the others, too, that being locked up within the boundaries of Nowhere County had better be a *brief*, unexplainable phenomena. It needed to vanish back to wherever it had come from *soon*, because if it hung around, there'd be severe consequences — and not just in missed dental appointments or a foiled trip to Walmart.

While Reece lay incapacitated by a splitting headache and a bloody nose, Grace recovered from vomiting quickly enough that she piled in beside Sam and Charlie tending to the "wounded," brushing off Sam's urging to sit down and take it easy with, "Don't be ridiculous, child, I'm in better shape than ninety percent of the people for a hundred yards in every direction."

Sam caught Charlie's eye when she saw Grace, nodded toward Pete Rutherford and whispered, "Pete takes weekly chemotherapy treatments in Lexington. Cancer. He's in remission now. But if he stops taking the treatments ..."

When Abner Riley recovered his vision, he hung around to help. Abner had a cleft palate and at some time in his life, somebody — and probably *not* a doctor — had sewn up the split lip part of the condition but left the rest. He had been an orderly in the hospital in the Ridge before it closed and was on his way to work in the hospital in Carlisle.

Thelma Jackson got her nosebleed under control pretty quickly and she stayed, too. Even taller than Sam, Thelma had been a high school history teacher — back when the Ridge had a high school — whose hobby was genealogy. Hers was one of only a handful of black families in the county. Her husband, Cotton, had played football for the University of Kentucky years ago and now commuted to Lexington six days a week to work as a foreman in a sewing machine factory. She was glad he hadn't been with her ... the Jabberwock and all. He had high blood pressure.

Other people stayed, too. A few. Rodney Sentry, a pig farmer. Roberta Callison, who raised chickens and sold eggs at a roadside stand. It didn't escape Charlie's notice, and it didn't surprise her, either, that the ones who stayed to help out were generally folks who had managed to make life work *somehow* in Nowhere County. The majority of the people transported by the Jabberwock to the parking lot were like most of the rest of the population of the county — they lived on government checks and food stamps, expected a handout and felt entitled to it.

As the day wore on, it became clear that the delivery truck that didn't show up that morning to deliver disposable diapers to the Dollar General Store had been a harbinger of things to come. The rural mail carriers didn't show. Rodney Sentry'd been waiting for delivery of a hog he'd bought from a farmer in Drayton County. Since the fellow didn't answer the phone, Rodney'd decided to go see what'd happened to him. Roscoe Tungate and his twin brother, Harry — as alike as two ears of corn picked out of an Iowa cornfield — were waiting for their cousin to bring them four cases of beer from Lexington, and when he didn't show up … the list went on and on.

Clearly, the Jabberwock gate to the world was locked on both sides.

Nobody could leave. Nobody could come in, either.

Abby Clayton had taken that understanding hard. She'd been counting on somebody to swoop in and rescue her so she could go get her baby. Charlie felt sorry for the young woman, even though if looks could kill, Charlie would have been pushing up daisies, courtesy of the daggers Abby was firing at her. It was unnerving, but about the middle of the afternoon, she noticed that Abby was nowhere to be seen. Someone must have given her a ride home.

In truth, there was really nothing anybody could do to help the people who'd lost a battle with the Jabberwock. All Sam, Charlie, Malachi, E.J., Liam, Pete, Grace, the Tungate brothers and the handful of others could do was get them cleaned up — as best they could — and keep the place hosed down — as best they could — and make them as comfortable as possible until the symptoms abated on their own.

Liam had summoned the volunteer fire department and they'd come roaring out of the Ridge, lights flashing and siren screaming. They likely didn't get an opportunity to do that very often and they took advantage of the thrill whenever they could. They were, after all, volunteers, summoned by beepers from the fields where they were milking cows, the backyard where they were hanging clothes on the line or the fry kitchen at A Salt and Battery, the fish and chips place in Twig. They operated the dilapidated equipment that would be used until it fell apart, and then so would the department because there were no funds to replace it. They had arrived and hooked a hose to the fire hydrant behind the Dollar General Store, and then helped to keep the parking lot and the bus shelter hosed down and as sanitary as possible. Luckily the strip mall had been built on a hill and the water off the lot ran down the nearby ditch and into the creek and was carried away.

At the peak of the festivities in the parking lot, Charlie did a rough head count and figured there were probably fifty people there — on a scale from just arrived and desperately sick all the way through to borrowing E.J.'s phone to summon transportation back home.

It was a rowdy crowd — angry, confused, sick and scared. And mountain people weren't accustomed to exercising much control over how they expressed themselves.

Women screamed and sobbed. Men yelled and cursed. Everybody demanded to know what was going on and nobody had any answers for them.

By late afternoon, the crowd had thinned out considerably — partly because there were fewer and fewer "incoming," courtesy of the telephone grapevine, which had first broadcast notice of the Jabberwock, and was now communicating the dire consequence of challenging the beast. And partly because those who came to see the "appearing" were fewer and didn't tend to stay as long. Maybe it was the stink. Charlie was just about used to it, but still when the breeze blew uphill from the creek it was ghastly.

That many people, that sick … it wasn't a scene most folks would choose to hang around and examine for very long.

It was early evening when Charlie heard Sam cry out, "Oh, Abby, no!" She turned to see Sam kneeling beside a figure on her hands and knees heaving, blood spewing from her nose, clearly an "incoming." It was Abby Clayton.

Chapter Twenty-Three

Malachi Tackett looked out over the Dollar Store parking lot as the last rays of the sun fired out over the top of Little Bear Mountain to the west. "Sunset" for mountain people was a gradual thing, a lengthening of shadows in the valleys and hollows as the sun dipped below the horizon out there on the flat.

The sounds of low voices. Someone being violently sick. Somebody else crying and a general moaning sound that seemed to come from everybody and nobody at the same time.

Not a whole lot different from a battlefield. Except nobody here was dying.

And he hadn't killed any of them.

He wasn't sure when it'd started, when the outline had formed. Boot Camp? When he shipped out? After the first exchange of gunfire? The first dead body? The first massacre? It was suddenly just there, a black edge, a frame that encased his reality, that surrounded his world from the moment he opened his eyes in the morning until whatever happened that day was done. Like somebody had outlined the life of Malachi Tackett in black Magic Marker. Some-times the frame closed in on him, somehow got thicker and thicker until the world that existed outside of it was small, a little circle, like looking at reality through a pipe.

And then the pipe would slam shut altogether, and when he opened his eyes he would be somewhere else entirely.

Now the frame was gone.

He didn't remember when it'd left, either. He'd been too busy to notice, but it was definitely gone.

Oh, everything else was still there, lined up for his inspection like recruits on the parade ground. The para-noia. But it wasn't paranoia until you came home. Until then, everybody really *was* trying to kill you.

Or how he worked out in his head how he'd get out of every situation he found himself in. Walking to the mailbox with Mama … how he could leap over that hedge and make a run for the tree.

Or how he could drop the mailman — *the guy in a mail-man's uniform* — grab his satchel with the bomb inside and throw it over the fence.

So many of the gifts that keep on giving he'd brought home with him from the war were still very much in evidence, thank you very much. But the frame was gone.

The black line did not surround the parking lot of the Dollar General Store in the Middle of Nowhere on that June Saturday night in 1995 and that was a thing of profound mystery and wonder for Lance Corporal— No! *Not* corporal. Just Malachi. Plain old Malachi Tackett.

He looked out at a world without a frame and was awed by its absence and by … how much less threatening an unframed world was.

The air smelled vaguely of vomit, though the fire brigade had done a yeoman's job of keeping the parking lot cleared of yuk, under the direction of Pete Rutherford who ruled it with an iron hand, making it clear, to Malachi at least, that the man had served in the military, had directed men there, had certainly sent them into battle to die.

And maybe understood.

He had, after all, talked Malachi back into reality when he believed he was pinned down by … as he crouched behind a bus shelter in a parking lot in rural Kentucky, his mind reverberating inside his skull like a ball in an oil drum.

He'd have a conversation with Pete when … after …

Malachi smiled, knew it was inappropriate but reveled in its inappropriateness. Malachi didn't give a rat fart about the Jabberwock. It didn't matter to him what it was. And he was probably the only person — out of the hundreds of people who'd experienced the phenomena in one form or another today — who didn't care. It seemed to him so insignificant in the grand scheme of things. In a world where hundreds of thousands of innocent people were butchered, hacked apart, their bodies piled up and left to stink by the side of the road … in a world where things like that were such a daily occurrence that *nobody even noticed,* an impossible phenomenon like the Jabberwock was no big deal at all.

He still felt a little lightheaded, had put nothing back in his stomach since he'd violently expelled its contents hours ago, but he also attributed some of the wooziness to the thing, the event, that started in the shadow of Bald Ridge and propelled him to a parking lot twenty-three miles away in …

How long had it taken?

That was something nobody'd thought to investigate, though he was sure every possible bit of minutia relating to the phenomena would be talked and examined and taken apart and dissected ad nauseam when it was over.

"I feel like I've got a hangover," said Liam Montgomery, who'd stepped up unnoticed beside Malachi.

Malachi jumped. Just jumped, though. Like anybody would. No over-reaction.

"Me, too. Like there's a …"

"Buzzing behind my eyes."

"Yeah, like that. Coming off a drunk."

"I've never felt a pain like that needle in my head, though, not ever before in my life, and I'd just about die to keep from ever feeling it again." Liam seemed very young then, and Malachi noticed that the deputy was probably five years younger than he was, which made him mid-twenties.

"Meaning you have no desire to step again through the mirror of the Jabber—"

That's when they both heard Sam cry, "Oh, Abby, no," heard the poor woman retching violently and knew that Abby Clayton had ridden the bronco a second time.

Sam held Abby Clayton's head while she heaved and retched, her body wracked by contractions in her diaphragm as strong as labor pains.

The girl was vomiting blood, too, and Sam had only seen one other person all day who'd done that — Betty Hannaker. She'd been on her way to Walmart to buy a plunger because her toilet was stopped up. And Betty'd only vomited a small amount of blood. Abby was vomiting nothing but blood after she'd expelled her stomach contents.

And her nose was bleeding, too.

If this had been a normal world and this had been anywhere in the same UPS delivery zone as a normal day, Sam would have dialed 911 and had Abby transported immediately to the hospital by ambulance.

She froze for a moment, a cold chill making its way down her back, dripping like ice water from one vertebra to the next.

That was a perfect word picture of the state of the world in Nowhere County Kentucky on June 3, 1995.

When you dialed 911, nobody answered.

Malachi came up beside Charlie, nodded to Abby and pointed out the obvious. "She didn't get a ride home after all."

She noticed as she spoke to him that his eyes had cleared. The effects of the Jabberwock had mostly worn off for him, but he also seemed more engaged with reality than he'd been before. In fact, he'd seemed to become more "normal" as the nightmare day went on.

While Charlie was getting wrapped tighter and tighter, Malachi Tackett was relaxing.

Charlie went to Sam and put her hand on her shoulder and she looked up, glanced pointedly down at Abby and shrugged her shoulders.

"How about I go get a wet cloth for you to—"

At the sound of Charlie's voice, Abby's head jerked up, spewing a fine spray of blood over Charlie's pants and shoes, the ones from the Dollar Store which she'd changed into because her jeans and Italian leather ballet flats had gotten to such a state they were unsalvageable. She'd have to burn them.

"Get away from me!" Abby snarled, coughing blood, her voice ragged.

"I'm sor—"

"Don't you touch me, you witch." Her words were garbled because she was forcing sound through vocal cords while her esophagus was responding to a greater imperative to vomit. "You brung it down on us—"

She couldn't finish then, her throat clogged with vomit and blood and she lowered her head and spewed it on the ground. Charlie backed away, reading a look of sympathy in Sam's eyes.

A hand on her shoulder patted kindly and she turned to see the benevolent wrinkled face of Pete Rutherford.

"Ain't no thang, sugar," he said, his accent comforting in a way she didn't bother to pick at. "It's just the Jabberwock."

Right. Everything that was wrong with her whole world and with the lives of everyone for twenty-five miles in every direction lay at the feet of the impossible phenomena of the Jabberwock.

Chapter Twenty-Four

It got dark, but still people came. Willingly or otherwise, they came.

Charlie had felt fatigue settling around her like a shroud for the past hour or so, a kind of tired unlike any she'd ever felt before. Maybe part of it an aftermath of the Jabberwock, because she still felt "off" somehow, had ever since she'd sat on the bench of the bus shelter at nine o'clock this morning. Correction, *yesterday* morning. It was long past midnight now.

Yesterday morning had been a lifetime ago.

Not a metaphorical description of the passage of time.

Literal.

It really had been a lifetime ago, and once she had the chance to consider all the ramifications of that, she would likely go nuttier than a squirrel turd. *Squirrel turd?* Where did *that* come from? The acclaimed children's author C.R.R. Underhill would never have thought a thing like ... just let it go.

She was just beginning to consider "what now?" What do you do after a day like this? Tell the gang how much fun you've had and let's do this again sometime real soon, and collect her daughter and go ...

Yeah. Go ... how? In truth, her mother's house wasn't very far away. Maybe a couple of miles *as the crow flies*, up over Little Bear Mountain and down the other side. The house was snuggled up against the mountain so tight there was hardly any room for a backyard. But Barber's Mill Road was like all the other small roads in the county, it meandered through the hollows and around the mountains. It went west from her house around the base of Little Bear and connected with Danville Pike a couple of miles west of the Middle of Nowhere.

And she no longer had a car. No, actually, she did have a car — her mother's that was parked in the driveway where Merrie had tripped over the downed tree limb. A 1991 Honda Legend. Ever-practical Mama.

What Charlie didn't have anymore was the rental car. The 1995 Chrysler Cirrus she had rented at the Lexington Airport. Well, right now it didn't seem likely she was going to be returning the car by the deadline. She'd have to pay a late charge. Bummer.

"Maybe it's time you went home," said a voice from behind her and she turned to see Sam surveying the ruins around them. Sam had already dispatched Pete, telling him several hours ago to leave if he "wanted to live until Christmas," which was obviously some kind of private joke.

"You got a little girl to put to bed."

Merrie McClintock was very likely the only human being in the whole of Nowhere County who'd had a great day. The receptionist in E.J.'s clinic claimed the child as her "assistant," and Merrie had spent the day with the animals. She'd played with the kittens and the puppies, helped feed the Labrador retriever who'd stayed the night after having an infected toe surgically removed. And with Mrs. Throckmorton, who had brought her cat into the clinic while Sam was still sitting in the waiting room there. The cat, whose name was Mittens, had been scheduled to have hairball surgery this afternoon, but that didn't happen. Mrs. Throckmorton had stayed on at the clinic, becoming Merrie's new best friend as the they hung out together. Every time Charlie went to check on her, Raylynn Bennett and Mrs. Throckmorton had waved her away with "she's fine." Every time Merrie saw her mother, she'd looked stricken, fearing that Charlie intended to take her away from her private menagerie.

But as evening turned to night, even the little powerhouse ran out of gas. Raylynn had settled her with a blanket and a couple of kittens on the wide bench in the reception area and she'd gone to sleep in seconds.

"What about you?"

"Do I have a little girl to put to bed? No. Or if I do, I don't remember where I left her."

"I *mean* what about you *going home*. You're bound to be more tired than I am."

Malachi stepped up as they were talking.

"Sounds like we're playing 'Can you top this,'" he said. "If we are, I'm here to report that I think I had the gold medal winner from the Olympic projectile vomiting team. That guy could—"

He must have seen the looks on their faces and faltered.

"I'm sorry." He sounded very tired indeed then. "Black humor. It's a way of coping. And ..." There was the suggestion, just the suggestion of a smile then. "If my actions at the bus shelter this morning, defending the bench against all enemies both foreign and domestic, is any indication, I'm no expert when it comes to coping skills."

Sam did smile; it was wan, but it was genuine. "I'll be

glad to run you home. Rusty's at a friend's house and he's spending the night."

Rusty must be Sam's little boy. Charlie didn't even know Sam had one, and a husband, too, maybe, for that matter. There hadn't been a whole lot of time for idle chit-chat.

Harry Tungate approached, worry etched in his face alongside the fatigue.

"Anybody seen Abby?" They shook their heads. "She's gone, and dollars to doughnuts she got somebody to take her to the county line."

Sam looked stricken. "She can't! She was so sick. We have to …"

"No telling who she caught a ride with," said Malachi.

Sam turned to Charlie.

"I need to get you and Merrie home and get back here. Abby's not going to be in good shape when she shows up."

Sam waited with Malachi outside E.J.'s office door while Charlie went in to get Merrie. Just standing there with him, not saying anything, should have been awkward, but they were both too tired and wrung out for awkward. They'd battled the Jabberwock today and the dragon took no prisoners.

In the lights the fire department had set up in the parking lot, they could see that the number of people showing up had finally dwindled to a trickle, either because it was so late or because word had spread that riding the Jabberwock was not like riding a rollercoaster, even if the resultant puking your guts up afterward was a similar effect.

"What *is* the Jabberwock, Malachi?" Sam said, and

instantly hated the pathetic, little-girl quality in her voice. She hadn't planned to say anything.

"I think the general consensus is some kind of bizarre meteorological phenomena blown in by the storm last night."

"Is that what *you* think?"

"No."

That surprised her.

"You don't? Then what do you think?" He didn't reply, just looked out past her at the parking lot. "Is it going to go away, vanish just like it appeared?"

He looked at her then, really looked at her for maybe the first time all day. The scrutiny brought instant color to her cheeks that the darkness blessedly covered.

"You're scared, aren't you?"

She hadn't been expecting the question.

"Shows, huh?"

He put his hand on her arm, a companionable gesture.

"Look around. If you're *not* scared right now, you are definitely not paying attention."

"I think—" Sam began, but the door opened and Charlie appeared, carrying a sleeping Merrie, so she stopped talking.

"Don't worry about waking her up," Charlie said. "We could drag her behind the car all the way home and it wouldn't wake her up. And that's on a day when she actually got to take two naps, which she didn't today. She could sleep through a nuclear attack."

Charlie turned to Malachi.

"E.J.'s looking for you to give you a key to the building, doesn't want to lock away your rifle."

Malachi had set his rifle inside E.J.'s reception area, behind the front door, when the group was loading up for the trip to the county line where Sam'd gotten her own ride on the Jabberwock.

The three just stood there then. Not knowing what to say and too tired to say it if they'd known. "Tomorrow …" Charlie began, and then fell silent.

"… will bring whatever it brings," Malachi said. "We'll deal with it."

"I have a car … Mom's car. The car the Jabberwock ate was a rental. I'll come back in the morning if …"

Again the words died, but they were unnecessary. If the world righted itself, the three of them might not see each other at all tomorrow … or ever again, for that matter. They'd just pick up where they'd left off and go on with their lives.

If it didn't … they'd all three be back.

Chapter Twenty-Five

Abby lay in the darkness, curled in a ball, in pain everywhere but nowhere in particular. It hadn't worked, the last attempt to leave, to get past the county line. Buddy and Mary Jo Cawdrey had brung her out. They lived up in the holler behind her granny's house and they was good folks and they'd been glad to give her a ride. Didn't neither one of them get there by way of the Jabberwock, so they wasn't sick, and Abby said she's just going out to the line to meet Ralph, her older brother, who was gonna pick her up there.

It hadn't been a very convincing lie but they never asked how come he was fetching her way out there, and it didn't matter if she'd talked them into it or no. If they hadn't took her, somebody else would have. She'd a walked if she'd had to. She'd a crawled.

The Cawdreys was smoking weed — offered her some, but she said no, that she was nursing. Or should have been.

While Buddy and Mary Jo giggled in the front seat of their little Chevy Chevette, Abby sat in the backseat readin' what she'd wrote up in that little notepad she always carried in her hip pocket. Her promises to God. Wasn't strictly true that she was readin' it, not with her eyes, anyway. Her pants had got wet, had blood and vomit on them, and she'd changed into Dollar Store hospital scrubs hours ago. But when she'd tried to pull that notebook outa her wet jeans, it'd come apart in her hand. Didn't matter. She didn't need them pieces of paper. She could read it with her memory and with her heart. She had ever word memorized.

They all started the same way: "God, if you'll let my baby live, I'll …" And the biggest one of all, the most important one was she'd swore she'd take good care of Cody, that she wouldn't never let no harm come to him. Now he was lyin' in a bassinet in a hospital up Lexington, crying, hungry, and she wasn't there to do for him like she'd swore she would be.

She was here, behind the bus shelter, lying in the dark, hurting everywhere, but she was glad of it. She understood that she'd had to go back through that third time so the Jabberwock could talk to her, whisper in her ear.

Hadn't nobody seen her yet, lying all scrunched up in the shadows. They'd set up lights so bright they blinded you so you couldn't see what was in the dark. She lay there listening to that Ryan woman, that witch, talk about her little girl.

The other reason hadn't nobody noticed her all curled up there was because she was quiet, she wasn't moanin' or screamin' or cryin' or puking and the like. And she knew why that was, too, why she wasn't sick. She understood everything because the Jabberwock had explained it all to her.

Somewhere in her registered a needle point of pain in the center of her skull that if she'd let herself notice it, it would have hurt so bad she'd a died right there from the hurt of it. Some other part registered that her joints hurt, her elbows and hips and knees. Ached like that time she'd sprained her ankle and it'd swole up big as a cantaloupe. Every one of her joints felt like that now, but she didn't let herself know those things, because she'd been given a gift and if she let herself know about how her body was hurting, she couldn't do what she had to do.

She was curled up in a fetal position because that's the way her arms and legs was bent when she come back and she didn't have the strength yet to uncurl herself.

Her face felt funny, numb kind of, and she couldn't see good out her left eye. Her nose was bleedin'. Her left ear was bleeding, too. Dripping off her face and down her neck to stain the Mickey Mouse scrubs she'd changed into after she puked on what she'd been wearing. Them scrubs was wet between her legs, too. She was bleeding … there, where Cody'd come out. She'd quit bleeding there while he was still in the intensive care unit and hadn't got her period since. They said it was 'cause she was nursing … well, pumping. The bleedin' there now didn't have nothing to do with her period, though. But it wasn't no thang.

Didn't nothin' matter except what the Jabberwock itself had said, a monster with eyes of flames, terrible-er than any nightmare. She liked to a died just being up close, it stinkin' like a rotting corpse, so close she could hear it whispering to itself, all them screechy voices that tore up her insides and made her ears bleed with the sound of silent screaming.

Mostly, it talked in that monster language Fish'd used in the backseat of the van — slighy toves that gyred and gimbled in the wabe — like that. 'Bout horror creatures — a Jubjub bird and a mome rath.

That's why Fish knew its name, because Fish was one of *them*, a bandersnatch, maybe. He'd knowed what was going on all along, but didn't matter now because she'd heard the Jabberwock say the witch from out there on the flat was why it was here. Said it'd been waiting for her, wanting her to come and play, her and the others.

And it'd stay here 'til she paid some attention to it. Like a dog waiting for a treat. A day, a week, a month.

But Abby's Cody wasn't gonna wait no week for his mommy to come get him!

Then Abby'd membered what Fish had said, about cutting the Jabberwock's head off with that sword. That vorpal sword.

That woman bein' a witch and all, you know she had a sword. All them magical creatures had swords and staffs and capes and the like. And soon's Abby figured that part out, she knew what to do. Abby would *make* that witch woman kill the Jabberwock with that sword. She would *hurt* that woman and that little girl of hers if she refused. She'd *kill* that child, if she had to. That mother didn't deserve no child when she was keeping Abby from hers.

Abby promised in her heart to make the witch slay the monster with flaming eyes — or die in the tryin' of it.

"Look over here," someone said, and she knew they'd seen her. Maybe they'd help her up, help her uncurl her arms and legs. She didn't care if they had to break her arms to get them free, she had to stand up. She had to walk. She had to hurry. She had a long way to go and her baby boy was hungry.

Chapter Twenty-Six

When Sam pulled back into the Dollar General Store parking lot after she took Charlie home, she saw Malachi deep in conversation with Thelma Jackson and some man she couldn't place. He was one of the Tungate boys from Solomon Hollow, she thought, had been one of the few folks who'd shown up out of curiosity, then stayed on to help out. Then Malachi turned and went into E.J.'s office.

Thelma hit her with the news as she was getting out of her car.

"Abby came back through."

And she was dead, that's what Sam thought. She'd got so sick she ... she'd bled to death ... internal bleeding or ...

"Where is she?"

"We don't know," said the Tungate who ran the butcher shop in Foodtown ... *Roscoe*. "She was here and then she wasn't."

"You mean she came back through the Jabberwock and then got up and walked away?" Sam was incredulous.

"I don't know about the walking part," Roscoe said.

"Shape she was in, I'd have been stunned to see her stand up. But she musta because she ain't here."

"Tell me what—"

"About an hour ago, I seen her laying on the ground behind the bus shelter, all doubled up in a ball, looked like a pill bug. I don't know how long she'd been a laying there, just a little thing curled up in the shadow not making a sound. Malachi was busy helping Liam load that Bennett fella into a car. That man weighs three hundred if he weighs an ounce, so Liam went along with his wife to help her get him up the front porch steps. I went to see could I help Abby but she didn't want no help, just held up her hand, wanted me to pull her up."

Roscoe took a breath.

"Course she was a mess, maybe had a stroke or something. Her mouth was kind of droopy on the left side and her eyelid was hanging down like. But wasn't like she was paralyzed or nothing. She could move. Slow. But most everybody here's been slow at first, comin' back from it."

Thelma tired of the snail's-pace progress of the story.

"She stood up, said she needed to go home and would we find somebody to take her. But there was nobody here who'd have been willing take that girl home and just leave her there all by herself in the shape she was in."

"She was bleeding bad," Roscoe put in. "Not bad like she was gonna bleed to death or nothin'. Just bad because it was comin' outa … lotsa places. Her nose and her ears. Even her eyes. And … other places. She needed a doctor, or you — somebody to see to her."

Malachi came out of E.J.'s office and strode with purpose toward them. Something about his body language spelled trouble.

"She's not there," he said.

"She wanted to go into E.J.'s office to go to the bathroom," Thelma said, "so she went in and she never came back out."

"Then where is she?" Sam said, sensing there was more that Malachi wasn't saying. "What is it — tell me."

"I left my rifle, the one I was squirrel hunting with, behind the door in E.J.'s waiting room. She saw me put it there when we were loading up the van. Now, it's gone."

"What are you talking about?" Sam was totally flummoxed. 'You're saying this bleeding stroke victim went in there and stole your gun and … what? What for?"

Thelma spoke then. Her voice was soft, not trying to be quiet but because she didn't have enough air to speak any louder.

"She was babbling about 'the witch from out there on the flat.' Most of what she said made absolutely no sense — about a monster with flaming eyes that smelled like dead bodies all mixed up with words and phrases from the Jabberwock poem."

"Don't know how she could have knowed them kind of words," Roscoe interrupted.

Malachi silenced him. "Fish was quoting the poem in the van. Go on, Thelma."

"She said the Jabberwock was the witch's fault because it had come to play with her and the others and it would stay until it got what it wanted. And, *of course* a witch would have a sword, a *vorpal* sword — crazy nonsense like that."

"Brain damage," Sam whispered.

"She said she was going to force the witch to use the sword to cut off the Jabberwock's head, kill it so she could go see her boy."

Thelma's voice was soft but the words were as powerful as a shout. "She said she was going to *kill the witch* if she refused."

Sam's hand flew to her mouth.

"Charlie!"

They turned in unison to look at Little Bear Mountain. Charlie's mother's house was on the other side.

"She couldn't possibly climb …" Sam began but couldn't finish. Took a breath and tried again. "It's two miles if it's a foot, *up the side of a mountain*, through the bushes, over limbs and dead trees and then back down the other side. In the dark — without a flashlight."

"She's got a flashlight," Fish said. Fish had been in the background of everything that had been going on all day, couldn't "get a ride home" because he didn't have one. He had disappeared into the back of the Dollar General Store late in the afternoon and when Sam went to the back to get more paper towels, she smelled something like cherries. Cough syrup. Fish was curled up in a corner with a bottle, had gotten his alcohol where he could.

"I made myself a place on the floor in the back of the store and she came in the back door. So she must have gone out E.J.'s back door and come around. I asked if I could help …"

He shook his head.

"I shouldn't have done that because I scared her, jumping out at her like I did. She cried out something, sounded like 'Bandersnatch!' and raised the rifle, pointed it right at me. I backed off, said I just wanted to help, that's all. She said she didn't need my help, then she dug around until she found a flashlight, one of the big ones with the two C batteries. She took it and the gun and went back out the way she came in."

"We need to call Charlie, warn her," Sam said. "Tell her to lock her doors and stay inside, not open a door for anybody."

"Thelma, you do that," Malachi said. He looked at Sam. "Can I borrow …?"

"No, I'm driving." Sam slid back behind the wheel and Malachi got in beside her.

"Keep trying until she answers," he called out to Thelma as Sam pulled out of the parking lot. "Keep calling. Tell her to run, to hide."

Chapter Twenty-Seven

Charlie stood in the darkness just inside the door after Sam dropped her off, just stood there. Then realized Sam wouldn't leave until she saw a light, so she flipped the switch. Still she stood, listening to the crunch of tires as Sam pulled out of the driveway and drove away, almost not feeling the weight of Merrie, dead to the world in her arms.

She waited for a few seconds, long enough for Sam to get far enough away from the house that she couldn't see, then she reached over and flipped the lights back off so she could stand there in the dark, listening to the sound of silence roaring in her ears.

She and Sam had said almost nothing to each other during the ride to Charlie's mother's house. Both just stared out the windshield, their own thoughts imprisoning them in their own worlds, which right now were two fenced-in yards next door to each other. Each contained their own stuff that they weren't ready yet to share, and each too full of their own stuff to have room for anybody else's.

This was crazy. It couldn't be happening. It didn't happen. This was all an illusion or a hallucination or a dream she was going to wake up from, feeling Merrie's wet kisses on her cheek and probably cry from relief that the nightmare was over.

Twilight Zone stuff like this didn't happen to normal people. No, not normal people. Her mother'd always pointed out that "normal is just a setting on a dryer." Ordinary, then. Ordinary people did not fly out into nowhere and get transported—

The word "transported" brought a burp of sound, maybe stifled laughter, some sound that bespoke the absurdity of it all.

She was Charlene Renee Ryan McClintock, thirty-two years old, with a birthmark shaped like a smiley face on her tush, a cesarean section scar on her belly where doctors had intervened after nineteen hours of unproductive labor and saved her little girl's life. She had a dentist appointment next week to replace the filling that'd come out when she bit into a piece of chocolate pie — a piece of pie, for crying out loud — and if she didn't return *The Lion King* to Blockbuster by five o'clock on Monday, she'd be charged a late fee, which she knew was how they made their money — late fees. And she hadn't even watched it yet. It had sounded like something Merrie would love, an animated musical about a lion—

Her mind was ping-ponging. Frantically racing from one inane thought to another so she wouldn't have to think about—

She let out what sounded like one of Merrie-the-Drama-Queen's theatrical sighs. And when she drew the breath back in, there was just a whiff of … vomit.

And the whole thing slammed down around her with

the clanging of the cell door in the execution chamber of a prison.

She started across the dark room toward the hallway that led to the bedroom that'd been hers when she was a little girl. That was where Merrie was sleeping. It wasn't the smell of vomit. She was imagining that part even if the rest of it was real. She'd stripped Merrie down to her birthday suit and dressed her in new clothes at the Dollar Store — underwear, socks, shoes, everything — even though she had only been in the presence of the yuk, not dealing directly with it like the rest of them had. And she'd thrown away what the little girl'd had on, a pair of jeans and a Whitney Houston tee shirt, stained with the blood from her head wound. Charlie had loved the cute outfit — but not enough to wash it. Charlie was on her third, maybe her fourth set of scrubs, having tossed her own clothing, including — *especially* — her shoes, when they'd gotten too gross. In the spill of light from Sam's headlights when Charlie'd crossed in front of the car, she'd noticed that the scrub shirt had a pattern of some kind — little balloons or flowers or maybe smiley faces. She hadn't noticed it when she'd grabbed a random shirt off a hanger on a rack between the posts with M's on them. A popcorn synapse fired. She wouldn't let Sam pay for all the stuff they'd used today — likely every set of hospital scrubs, which would fit anybody, in the building and an uncountable number of towels and washcloths. The *real* hero of today's catastrophe would be whoever volunteered to wash all the dirty stuff … if anybody did. Probably best to take it out into the parking lot and burn it. Lunch and dinner, too, what little their unsettled stomachs would tolerate — peanut butter and jelly sandwiches, Vienna sausage, chips and, of course, Ding Dongs, HoHo's, Moon Pies and soft drinks. And paper goods — paper towels and paper cups and bottled water and … the list was huge. Everybody'd just taken what they needed. That was going to be quite a bill … but that was a thought for another day.

"Ouch!" she cried, hopping around on one foot after she banged her shin painfully on the coffee table.

There was a full moon but the curtains were drawn so she might as well have been in an oil drum, and she wasn't familiar enough with the current placement of the current furniture in her mother's house to negotiate a trip across the living room in the dark. She should have left the light on.

Making it to the hallway without further mishap, she felt along the wall for the light switch and turned it on, went all the way to the end, carrying Merrie into the bedroom on the front of the house she'd inherited years ago from her older sister, Mallory. Who'd married that idiot who fancied himself a boat captain and they'd taken Mama out—

Nope, not *there*, either.

The room had been redecorated … no that was too formal a term. Over the years, it had gradually been un-Charlied. The bed was the same — a huge four-poster oak cannonball that was so high off the floor her mother'd always been paranoid one of the girls would fall off and break her neck. And Charlie's old, threadbare bedspread and bed skirt remained — though they should have been replaced with the curtains and the wall art. Most people who knew Charlie now would have trouble believing it, but she had been a very "girly" little girl — all about ribbons and bows and pretty dresses and always, always, always *anything* ballerina. Her bedroom walls had been covered with ballerina art. The bedspread was a soft, pale pink chenille, and the bed skirt that stretched from the mattress to the floor was made of poufy pink organza, three stiff layers of it sticking out like the bed was dressed in a ballerina skirt.

Laying Merrie down on the bed, she flicked on the bedside lamp and started to undress her, then changed her mind. She untied her shoelaces and removed her new shoes. The kid could sleep in her clothes. They were clean. She didn't even pull down the sheets. She just picked up the Cracker Barrel quilt her mother'd bought with a tag that claimed it was handmade and maybe it had been, and snuggled the child up under it. Then she went to the window, unhooked the latch and raised it a couple of inches to let the room air out. It was stuffy. The house had been closed up when she'd arrived and it still smelled musty. She'd been systematically going from one room to the next boxing up anything that mattered, that she or Mallory might want to keep. She'd let the real estate agency handle everything else. She had planned to be finished in time to get the rental car back to the agency by five o'clock even though her flight wasn't until nine.

The best laid plans of mice and men …

She paused before she turned off the light, looking down at the sleeping child. Oh, to be able to turn the world off so completely like Merrie could!

Charlie didn't like admitting it, but with the wash of light and shadow over her face and the black curls, Merrie McClintock bore a striking resemblance to her father. She was biracial and that'd be an issue for her as she got older — though that kind of bigotry was blessedly fading out of American society. It wasn't that Charlie wanted to deny Merrie's African-American heritage. She would always help the child celebrate that. She just didn't like being reminded of the handsome ex-football player who had charmed her, swept her off her feet and then—

Why was her mind going to all the places Where the

Wild Things Are tonight? Maybe because her synapses were so fried that her automatic barriers had short-circuited and were down and all the stray cattle were now wandering out into the road.

She leaned over and planted a kiss on Merrie's plump cheek, then switched off the light, plunging the room into darkness before she closed the door. Since she never woke up in the middle of the night, Merrie did not require a nightlight.

Once Charlie had Merrie in bed, her sense of purpose left her and she stood in the hallway trying to think what she ought to do. A fog rolled in off the sea into her mind and nothing was distinct anymore. Everything had bright haloes and soft edges. Well, one thing she ought to do was call the rental agency at the airport and tell them their vehicle would not be returning as per their prearranged agreement. She picked up the receiver off the wall phone in the hallway before it occurred to her that she didn't know the number. It was printed on both the yellow and pink copies of the car rental agreement ... which she had stuffed into the glove box of the car ... which was ... where? Somewhere. Everything had to be somewhere.

She didn't have the phone number of the reservations department of American Airlines memorized either. It was on her plane ticket, which was in her purse, which was ...

Yeah, that.

She replaced the receiver heavily. What was she thinking? Clearly, nothing at all. How many people had tried to call "out" somewhere outside Nowhere County today? Every one of them encountered the same phenomenon. The phone never rang on the other end, but there was no busy signal either. The phone just went dead, like somebody'd snipped the wires. And somebody had. Some*thing*. The Jabberwock.

Going down the hallway to the "guest" bedroom on the back of the house, she flipped on the light and flounced in exaggerated fatigue, spread-eagled on the quilted bedspread, which might also have come from Cracker Barrel. She lay there as she'd fallen, feeling her exhausted muscles begin to relax, and considered following Merrie's lead. Just kick off her shoes and pull the bedspread over her. After all, her clothes were as clean as Merrie's.

But *she* wasn't clean. Didn't feel clean, at least. In fact, as soon as she thought about it she considered that maybe she had smelled vomit after all — on her body, her skin or … oh, gross, *her hair*.

She practically leapt up off the bed and went to the bathroom — the hall bath with its charming antique fixtures, not the one off her bedroom with a shower. She didn't want a shower; she wanted a *bath!*

The clawfoot bathtub was so big you had to drain the whole hot water heater to fill it to the top. Fine. That was just dandy. Charlie turned on the water, both handles, hot and cold, looked around, found a bottle of bubble bath and poured a more than generous portion into the water. The flower smell filled the room and Charlie inhaled it deeply. For some reason, the smell made her want to cry.

Chapter Twenty-Eight

Sam took the corner too fast and swerved into the oncoming lane, but she knew it was empty. If you were going to drive recklessly, too fast, suicidal fast, the mountains were the place to do it because you could see approaching headlights around corners and on the other sides of hills.

She didn't even glance at Malachi, sitting tense beside her, but knew he had to be concerned about their speed.

"I'm a good driver," she said without looking at him, regretting the words as soon as they left her mouth. What an absurd thing to say. Like he would believe her. Like it mattered.

They had to get to Charlie's before …

"You don't really think …?"

She let the question dangle, but he didn't answer it so she completed it. "You don't think Abby would actually … do something, do you?"

"Yeah, I do."

Her eyes snapped to him for a moment and then back to the road. The certainty of that statement.

"Why are you so sure?"

"Because her mind is ... because she's had a stroke. Maybe it's a stroke, but something's definitely screwed up in her head and I am here to testify that when something's screwed up in your head, there is absolutely nothing you won't do." Then he whispered softly, probably wasn't aware that he was speaking. "Absolutely *nothing*."

"But how could she possibly climb that mountain in the shape she's—"

"She could climb it."

She shot him a glance and he was looking at her now. "Same reason. You can do just about anything if you have to."

"Merrie ... she's just a baby. Abby's a sweet kid and she wouldn't hurt ..."

She looked at him and saw the same answer written on his face. The car fell silent. Sam could hear her own breathing sounding ragged in her throat and the pounding of her heart was surely hammering so fast each beat was visible on the front of her shirt.

"You were good out there today," he said.

She shot him a more-than-a-second look, then back to the road.

"You stepped up and ... we called it 'doing the necessary.' Means what it sounds. But not everybody's willing to do the necessary. You were."

"I wanted to become a doctor."

Where did *that* come from? Why in the world would she say a thing ... because it was true. She had wanted to be a doctor ever since she was a little girl. She was always taking the temperature of the baby dolls she and Charlie played with at recess every day. Bandaging their broken arms and legs, without giving a whole lot of thought, of course, to how a six-month-old infant had broken both arms and both legs.

"But you didn't."

"No, I didn't." She felt the need to go on. "Oh, I didn't mean it like people are always saying, 'I was always going to write a book someday.' I really would have—"

"I'm sure you really would have. But a coal miner's daughter ..."

"Not so much."

"You'd have been a good one."

She didn't know what to say to that so she didn't say anything at all.

"It's a good thing you're here now. Folks are going to need you."

That somehow had a sinister sound.

'You don't really think this thing—" she didn't like the word Jabberwock, but it did seem appropriate -- "this Jabberwock thing is going to *stay* here."

"And you don't?"

It NEVER FAILED. It was one of the great cosmic truths of life. As soon as you got into a bathtub, the phone rang.

That was the phone ringing, right? The bathwater was running, making so much noise Charlie couldn't be sure. Maybe it wasn't the phone. And if it was, they'd call back if it was important. Right now, Charlie had no intention of getting out of the tub and tippy-toeing little puddles down the hallway to answer it.

The tub was actually too big to be comfortable for a person her size. It was too long. If she leaned back against the back of the tub, her feet didn't reach the other end and she slid down into the water. But she'd figured a way around that when she was a kid, and she'd had to shoo away the bats and blow dust off memories to recall. Then she looked in the corner behind the tub and it was still there! After all these years, it was still there. As a small child, she'd used a little three-step plastic stool to reach the sink. When she got older, she'd set the feet of the plastic stool against the front end of the tub — then she could stretch out in the tub, lean against the back, put her feet on the stool and not drown.

She leaned back now, the rumble of water raising mountains of bubbles. The air smelled sweetly of lavender, or maybe violets. She wasn't up on her flower aromas like perhaps she should have been. It probably said on the bottle, but she was too relaxed to lift up and look at the bottle. As she lay in the warm water, the tension began to ease out of her muscles and the result was a rubbery sense that if she tried to stand, her knees probably wouldn't hold her upright.

Once the tub was full, she turned the water off and could hear the phone ringing again. Or still. If somebody was that determined to talk to her, it must be important. She began to consider getting out of the water when the ringing cut off abruptly. She settled back against the back of the tub. If it was all that important, they'd call back.

The main reason her mother'd had a shower installed in Charlie's bathroom was the issue of hair washing in the big clawfoot tub. You could get your hair wet, soap it up and get it clean, but the only way to rinse it was in the water you were sitting in. Well, if you were desperate for clean water, you *could* stick your head under the cold water spigot and get a brain freeze or under the hot water spigot and blister your scalp. One or the other. Pick.

Tonight, she'd be satisfied with clean hair, even if she wasn't able to get all the bubble bath out of it. And she'd best get to washing it soon, while she still could. Every speck of her remaining strength had melted into a puddle in the hot water and her exhaustion was palpable. She might have trouble getting out of the tub and making it to her bedroom.

Besides, the water was getting cold.

She rinsed her hair one more time, sinking down into the water and came back up spewing, then stood and grabbed the bath blanket off the rack beside the tub. It was not as soft as her own bath towels but she knew why. She could smell sunshine in the fabric, knew it'd been dried on the line in the backyard instead of in a dryer.

She dried off, and slipped into the pajamas and robe she'd grabbed out of her suitcase — which she had never unpacked.

Wiping the steam on the mirror off with the edge of the towel, she looked at her own reflection and quickly realized that wasn't a good idea. The words "death on a cracker" came to mind. What showed on her face was testimony to the reality of all she'd seen and experienced today and she really didn't want to be reminded.

Rigorously drying her hair with the towel — her hairstylist had warned against that. "You damage your hair when you rub your head with a towel like you're trying to buff a shine on a cherry red Mustang. Blot it dry."

Blot it. Not tonight. Charlie couldn't sleep with wet hair, had never been able to stand that. She opened the bottom cabinet beneath the sink, felt around and found the "mini blow dryer."

She leaned against the high side of the clawfoot tub, leaned her head over and began to dry the underside of her hair, shaking her head and running her fingers through the wet strands. Then she stood, shook her head and felt of her hair. Still damp. But good enough.

Stepping out into the hallway, she instantly regretted not getting her house shoes out of her suitcase along with her pajamas and robe. The hardwood floor felt cold on—

The telephone receiver in the hall was dangling down from the phone by its cord, hanging there about an inch from the floor. Swaying back and forth.

~

Sam was so surprised she didn't know how to reply. Did Malachi … could he actually believe the Jabberwock was anything other than a passing event, a mystery that'd probably never be solved? A conundrum.

"No! Of course, I don't think it'll be here long." She actually stammered out the words. "Why on earth would it—?"

"Have appeared in the first place? *That's* the sixty-four-thousand-dollar question."

"That nobody can answer. So why would you think that—?"

"I think it's permanent."

The words so totally knocked the air out of her lungs she had trouble formulating a sound and getting it out past her lips.

"Permanent?"

"Un huh. I don't think it's going away."

"Why? It makes a whole lot more sense that some freak meteorological thing caused by that wacko, Looney Tune storm yesterday somehow caused … oh, I don't know. I bet scientists are going to spend the next decade trying to figure it out. If they believe any of us when we tell them about it. And those kinds of things, storm things, they pass. Tornados don't hang around day after day for a week. Much less … forever. Why would you—"

"I don't think the Jabberwock has anything to do with yesterday's storm."

Now, *there* was a conversation stopper. Sam sputtered some sound, it wasn't a ladylike one whatever it was, some aborted expletive.

"Why on earth not? What other explanation could there possibly be?"

"Does not believing the storm explanation require that I come up with an alternative?"

"Well, no, but ... so you don't have any idea what *did* cause it, you just know what *didn't* — the storm?"

"Something like that."

"I don't understand ..."

"Neither do I. Look, I don't claim to know anything the rest of you don't know. It was just, me and Pete talked about it and ..."

"And ...?"

"And doesn't it bother you that nobody" — he made an all-inclusive gesture — "*out there* has noticed? People had places they were supposed to be."

He ticked them off, rapid-fire: "Abner was supposed to be at work. Timmy Bessinger had a dentist appointment. Liam radioed the Beaufort County Sheriff's Department to intercept the speeder and the speeder showed up but Liam didn't. Grace was supposed to have dialysis, Pete had a chemotherapy appointment. Roberta was a no-show at her own birthday party and you know how big her family is. Abby was supposed to pick up her baby!"

He ran out of steam then and continued slowly. "Those are just the ones we know about. None of those people showed up where they were supposed to be ... and *nobody came looking for them.* Why not?"

Of course Sam had thought about that, wondered about it. They all had. But they'd been too busy and —

admit it — too thunderstruck by it all, or maybe still too affected by what the Jabberwock had done to each of them individually to do much conjecturing.

Sam made a tire-sliding turn onto Barber's Mill Road where Charlie's mother's house sat at the base of Little Bear Mountain, and she had to focus all her attention on the road. And into that focused attention dropped an understanding her conscious mind was studiously ignoring. In truth, she thought Malachi might be right. From the very beginning, she'd sensed *something* about the phenomenon … a power. Reality was, Sam Sheridan didn't think the Jabberwock would go poof with a sparkle like a soap bubble and be gone. There was more to it than that. It would not be that easily beaten.

"When we get there," Malachi said, "I want you to wait in the car until—"

"I'm not waiting in the car. Charlie—"

"If Abby's here, she's got a gun."

"She wouldn't shoot *me*. I'm the one who—"

"She would shoot *anybody*. You don't really get this, Sam, and you need to. That woman is insane. She has reached the ragged edge of desperation and there's no turning back, nothing she won't do, nobody she won't kill. No boundaries of any kind."

"What makes you think she'll listen to *you* rather than—"

"*Listen?* You think I'm going in there to *reason* with Abby?" He shook his head and focused his gaze back out the windshield. "I'm going in there to take her out."

Chapter Twenty-Nine

Now *that* was exceedingly weird!

Charlie stood in the hallway, her bare feet on the cold hardwood, and stared at the receiver of the phone, swinging slowly back and forth. And for a moment a wave of fear washed over her, but then it retreated back out to sea.

She could have sworn she'd hung the receiver up when she'd almost called the rental car agency. But apparently she—

It was still swaying.

She'd been in the tub at least a half hour. Longer than that. Long enough for the water to get cold. Then dried her hair. So why was the receiver still moving if she'd dropped it before she even started running the bathwater?

And the phone had rung!

How could it have rung if it had been off the hook?

The wave of fear washed back up onto the shore.

It had rung! It *had* rung … hadn't it?

She thought it had, but even at the time she hadn't

been sure and now she had no idea if she'd imagined it or
…

Well, she had to have imagined it. Because off-the-hook
phones didn't—

Why was it still swaying, the receiver turning like that
guy who hung himself in Mr. Fischer's English class?
Loopy. She was getting loopy. The guy didn't hang himself
in Mr. Fischer's class. He'd hanged himself in the book Mr.
Fischer'd made them read. She couldn't remember
anymore the name of it, but she clearly remembered that
one image from it: a dead man, hanging at the end of a
rope, his body slowly spinning, facing the different points
on a compass — north, then east, then south, then west.
She'd always wondered what'd kept him spinning.

But the rope hadn't been an elastic extension phone
line. And you could probably dangle the receiver on the
end of one of those for three days and it'd keep twisting.

The phone had rung.

Maybe.

This was nuts. She cinched the robe ties tight around
her waist, marched down the hall, picked up the receiver
where it dangled and put it to her ear. The line was dead.
She pecked on the "thingy" — she'd never known what
that disconnection bar was called — a time or two. Still no
dial tone. It sounded dead, just like the phones sounded
when they'd tried today to call out of the county.

No, actually those phones had sounded *un*connected or
*dis*connected. This one had that hollow sound like the
phone in the kitchen was off the hook, too.

That thought grabbed hold of her guts and yanked
them as tight inside her belly as the rope tie on her robe on
the outside. Her thundering heart became a herd of stam-
peding buffalo. She—

Stop it! Just stop it.

She was tired, exhausted, had earned more than a few fried synapses.

Replacing the receiver in its cradle, she wiped her hand off on her robe and headed toward the front of the house to peek in on Merrie before she collapsed in glorious catatonia in the back bedroom. It had a feather bed. The anticipation was delicious.

She felt something sticky on the doorknob of Merrie's bedroom door and wiped her hand again on her robe, pushing the door into the darkness of the room, lit now only by the saber of light from the hallway. She crossed to Merrie's bed and stood for a moment, looking at the lump of a kid under the blanket. Sometimes she was ... what was it the Brits said? Gobsmacked. Yes, gobsmacked by how much she adored that child. She smiled, and as she turned back toward the lighted hallway, she glanced down at the front of her robe.

The smile drained off her face.

There was something smeared across her robe. Something black. But she knew that in good light the smear wouldn't be black. She knew exactly what color it would be. Red. Blood red.

She pivoted back toward the bed, moving like she was encased in that clear stuff they found prehistoric bugs in — amber. She watched her hand glide through the air to the top edge of the blanket, saw her fingers grasp it and pull it down.

All the oxygen was instantly sucked out of the room.

Merrie wasn't under the blanket on the top of the bed. The lump wasn't a little girl. It was a pillow and a doll. A bloody doll.

A voice spoke out of the shadows, a nightmare voice full of pebbles.

"She ain't there."

Charlie whirled toward the sound, unable to breathe or think.

Then she watched in horrified amazement as the shape stepped ... shambled out into the light. The figure was dressed in filthy, torn rags of clothing, a suit of scrubs from the Dollar General Store, but ripped, muddy and bloody. Her hair was a tangle with leaves and twigs. Looked like she'd been dragged through a mile of briars and brambles.

Her face was skeletal, and much as Charlie tried, she could not picture what Abby Clayton had looked like when she first saw her, fuzzy blonde hair, face still raw from very recent adolescent acne. But beautiful. Beautiful with hope and love and joy and excitement. That girl was a person life had smiled on.

This creature was none of those things. She was bleeding or had bled out of every orifice of her body. Small streams of blood, not gushing, but surely the accumulated blood loss ...

Bloody tears streamed down her filthy cheeks. Her ears were bleeding, as was her nose, and the crotch of the scrub pants was a wet, black stain.

She'd suffered some kind of stroke or brain bleed or something because the left side of her face wasn't lined up properly with the other side. She was clearly missing teeth, but maybe she had been before, too, and Charlie just hadn't noticed. Her voice was the sound of chains dragged across a metal floor. Cold and ragged and fearful in every way. The strip of light that sliced into the room from the hallway lit the fire of rage on her face. Sparkled in her eyes.

The left side of her body didn't appear to be affected by the stroke or whatever'd happened in her brain. She held the rifle firmly, finger on the trigger.

It took several gasps before Charlie had enough air to speak.

"Where's Merrie? What have you done with my baby?"

"Ain't 'bout where she is. It's 'bout where she ain't and she ain't where she's supposed to be." Abby took another shuffling step farther into the light. "Just like *I* ain't where *I'm* supposed to be — up Lexington with my boy."

"What have you done with—?"

"Shut up!"

The words rode a spray of blood out the creature's mouth.

"Ain't for you to be talkin'. You listen. You brung that monster down on us. Ain't no use denying it. I heard them whispering, the voices, saying the Jabberwock come to Nowhere County to play kiddie games with you and them others and have fun."

"What on earth are you talking—?"

"I said for you to shut your filthy witch's mouth!

Abby advanced another step.

"But you got yourself a sword, one of them 'vorpal blades' and you gonna use it on him. You gonna go looking for him in the woods behind that mirror thing where he hides. You gonna find him and kill him. Cut off his head — snicker snack — hold it up for everybody to see. Then everything'll go back to the way it's supposed to be and I can go get to my baby."

"Where is my little girl?"

Charlie was glad to hear there was neither fear nor pleading in her voice. It was made of pure, cold steel and the power of it unsettled Abby just a bit.

"Don't matter where she's at."

"Tell me what you did with my daughter." Charlie advanced a step, with no firm plan of what she was going to do, though she was aware that her fingers had formed unconsciously into claws.

"Wouldn't do that, I's you. I done planned for that part, you jumping me to get the gun and me too weak to fight back. That's why I done what I done, so you couldn't stop me by takin' my gun, so you'd *have to* do what I say. You don't and your little girl's gonna die."

Charlie started to take another step.

"I hid the key. Somewhere you'll never find it. Even if you get my gun, even if you kill me, without that key, you can't get that door open in time and yore little girl's gonna *suffocate*."

Charlie was so staggered by the words her mind cartwheeled, fired random thoughts with no meaningful connections.

"I put her in the kiln."

Charlie screamed, shrieked, wailed … without making a sound because sound required air and she couldn't breathe.

"Locked her up tight in there and hid the key. You best do what I tell you real quick, or she's gonna *die* in there."

Charlie's mind was processing as fast as she could. Merrie was … *in the kiln*. Locked inside it.

"No, you couldn't—"

"Could and did. My mama come here lotsa times when I's a kid, watchin' your mama make them pots and ashtrays and such. A cup that wouldn't sit flat on the table was all Mama made, but she told me all about your mama's art stuff. About the kiln and how it had to be airtight. How it was locked up, but your mama kept the key on a nail behind the door so she could get to it when she needed it. It was right there, when I felt around for it. Just like she said."

"You put my baby in the kiln *and closed the door?*" The magnitude of the horror was staggering.

"Didn't just close it. *Locked it.* She never made a peep. I come in the window, carried her out the back door and she never even wiggled."

It was incredible that the woman before her was even able to stand. How had Abby carried Merrie — that child was a little *chunk* — and ...? But how had Abby gotten here?

She'd *climbed the mountain!*

"Put her down real careful like on a piece of brand new carpet that was a layin' on top of a stack of carpet rolls on the floor."

Carpet. Her mother had carpeted her bedroom a couple of years ago, said the hardwood was too cold on her feet. Had she stored the leftover carpet in the kiln?

"I didn't want to wake her up and her start pitchin' a fit." She paused and the menace in her voice was chilling. "She'd a woke up ... it'd a got *ugly.* But that carpet was soft as a bed and you's right, that littlun sleeps like the dead. Which is what she's gonna *be* if you don't get her out of there 'fore she breathes up all the air."

All the air.

How much was there?

How much breathable air was in the kiln? Charlie had no idea. It was a big kiln, but it wasn't *empty.* Her mother had used it for storage after she closed up her pottery shop, put all her art supplies in it. And there was other stuff in it, too, seemed like. It'd been years since Charlie'd been inside, but she knew there were boxes, big boxes sitting everywhere. Shoot, the Christmas tree decorations were even stored in it.

"I'm thinking an hour — no, more like an hour and a half. Hard to know because that kiln was jammed full of all kind of stuff. Wasn't hardly no place to lay her down, but she ain't big as a miner, so she wouldn't use up as much air. Outside'd probably be two hours, but I surely would *not* count on that."

This was a coal mining community. Everybody knew the "math of life," the formula that determined what happened after a mine cave-in — whether there was enough air in the tunnel to last until rescue came.

Abby recited it: "One cubic yard of air will last one miner one hour. That's the onliest reason my daddy learned the multiplication tables." Height, width and length multiplied together and divided by twenty-seven. "The 'divided by twenty-seven' part's the hardest, so you change it to thirty and you's close enough. Take the zeroes off the end of it and the other number and you's just dividin' by three. Ain't hard. Anybody can do that."

Charlie finally found her voice.

"You can't possibly be serious, you'd leave a little girl closed up in—"

"Would and did. She ain't been in there more than five minutes. You still got lotsa time."

Charlie looked at her watch. It was 2:51 a.m. Abby had locked Merrie in the kiln at 2:45, then. In an hour, it would be 3:45. In an hour and a half, it would be 4:15 a.m. In two hours, it would be 4:45.

"It don't take but what? Twenty minutes to get from here to the county line? Round trip's forty minutes and you got sixty — maybe ninety. You take me, use that Vorpal Sword on the monster and make him let us go—"

"I will not leave my baby—"

"I left *my* baby. Left him up there in the hospital waiting for his mama to come nurse him. But I'm comin' now. Half an hour from now I'm gonna be on my way to Lexington to get him."

On her way *how?* Was she planning to walk? In her condition? Hitch a ride? Wasn't a whole lot of traffic in the middle of the night on a desolate mountain road. Then Charlie knew. Abby planned to kill her and take her car.

"Ever second you spend standin' here jawin' your girl's usin' up air in that kiln. We need to git."

Charlie surrendered. A clock was ticking. She'd think of something.

"Okay."

"Keys is in your mama's car. I done checked. I checked everything. Climbin' that mountain, I had lotsa time to plan what I's gonna do."

Chapter Thirty

Malachi was impressed that Sam could keep the old car on the road. But she obviously knew the car like a best friend and the road just as well. She anticipated the curves, watched for lights around bends, slowed just a bit before the whoop-de-dos so that flying up into the air and banging back down didn't send them off into a ditch.

As the day'd worn on, he'd been more and more surprised at his own reaction to the insanity, the craziness that he might just wake up tomorrow morning in some Veteran's Hospital somewhere to discover was all an allergic response to some drug.

He'd felt calm and centered and understood that was because the situation put him back into his element, the emotional space where he felt most comfortable. He functioned well "doing the necessary" and there'd been a lot of that today. And he'd felt the coiled spring inside him begin to uncoil, not all the way, but enough to allow him more rational thought than he'd had since he got home at Christmas. He was enormously grateful for that, because it was with a clear head that he'd decided he would very likely have to kill Abby Clayton. He hated that, but it would be "doing the necessary." He wouldn't have left that decision up to Liam, even if Liam'd been there to come with them. But it'd be nice to be packing the deputy's sidearm.

The spring began to recoil itself as they turned off Danville Pike onto Barber's Mill Road and headed down it to the home of Sylvia Ryan, Charlie's mother. As soon as Sam squealed into the driveway, he grabbed her forearm and squeezed, probably so tight it hurt but that was okay.

"We agreed. You stay here."

"I didn't agree to anything. But it doesn't matter. She's not here. Sam's mother's car was parked in the driveway when I brought her home. Now it's gone."

"I said, stay here."

She didn't argue with him, but neither did she make any move to get out of the vehicle.

"Kill the lights."

She killed the lights.

He got out of the car, careful not to close the door with a sound that could be heard. Then he Groucho-walked to the side of the house next to the front door and flattened himself up against it. Exposing as little of his body as possible, he peeked carefully around the frame of the window, but the interior of the room was dark and he could see nothing but shapes and shadows.

His plan, such as it was, was to jump Abby the moment he saw her. Take advantage of surprise and the fact that she couldn't move fast. Crash down on her instantly before she had time to shoot. But if she saw him coming, if he couldn't surprise her, Plan B was to trick her, somehow, to get that one moment of inattention, and dive for the rifle.

It was surprisingly hard to deliver a lethal wound to a moving target with any weapon, no matter how *NYPD Blue* made it appear. She'd be firing a .22. It was for hunting squirrels and it'd be hard to kill a man with a single shot from a .22. Could be done, if you hit a vital organ, but he'd be moving fast and the odds were on his side that even if she shot him, he'd survive the wound — at least long enough to take her out.

He went around the house to the back, ducking under the windows so he couldn't be seen. The gate to the backyard fence was standing ajar. The back door was unlocked. He was tempted to call out for Charlie, but there went his element of surprise, so he eased the screen open just enough to squeeze through. The spring on every screen door on the planet squeaked when you opened it all the way, even if you slathered it in WD-40. He crossed the dark kitchen and ventured into the hallway. He smelled flowers, some kind of flowered perfume, soap or bubble bath maybe. He checked the rooms systematically, cleared them one by one, and found what he was looking for but hoping not to find in the room on the front of the house. The window was up and there was blood on the window sill. Instead of a little girl in the bed, there was a doll — with blood on it. Blood on the floor, too, drips that lead out the front door. He followed the drips out the door and ran to the car.

"They're gone. There was a bloody doll lying in the little girl's bed."

"*Merrie!*" Sam sucked in a gasp. "Abby thinks Charlie can kill the Jabberwock. What's she going to do to Charlie and Merrie when she finds out different?"

"Let's hope we get there before she does."

Instead of putting the car in reverse, Sam opened her door and leapt out of the car, flinging "Wait!" over her shoulder as she raced into the house. She returned in seconds, carrying a bundle that she tossed into the front seat.

"What's—?"

"A bluff."

Chapter Thirty-One

It was all Charlie could do to keep from screaming. She wanted to leap across the car and grab the madwoman by the throat, choke her, force her to tell what she'd done with the key.

Merrie was locked in the kiln.

The kiln!

She would die if Charlie couldn't get her out before the air ran out.

Somewhere inside she did scream, she shrieked, though she made no audible sound. She wailed in terror and impotent rage, wailed at the top of her psychic lungs. But she remained silent.

And when she finished screaming she grabbed hold of her emotions and grasped them in an iron-claw grip. If she panicked, Merrie would die. If this woman killed Charlie, Merrie would die.

She had to think of something, some way to get this crazy monster to tell her what she had done with the key.

But how?

The tatters of her mind blew in circles, like the black

flanks of starlings that cavorted over the trees, thousands of them, turning in unison, diving and soaring back and forth across the invisible Beaufort County border. Her thoughts were those starlings. They were dark, thousands and thousands of them, too many to pick out any one of them to think.

What could she do? Once they got to the county line and Abby realized Charlie had no magical sword to use on the Jabberwock, what would Abby do?

No, more important, what would Charlie do? She would have no choice but to jump Abby, wrest the rifle out of her hands and then …

Then what?

Threaten to shoot her if she didn't tell where the key was? Abby would know that was a bluff. What else could she do? How could she make Abby give her the key to the kiln?

The airless kiln where her baby lay in the darkness.

The scream on hairy black legs tried to crawl up the back of her throat and threatened to leap out of her mouth but she fought it back.

She prayed Merrie was still asleep. That she hadn't awakened and found herself in the dark, the absolute darkness of a cave or a coal mine. Alone and in the dark, oh please no! Not her little Merrie.

She sucked in a sob at the thought.

"Makes you sad, don't it — thinking 'bout your baby a hurtin'."

"Abby, *you're* hurt, can't you see that? The Jabberwock made you sick and—"

"I ain't too sick to go get my boy. He needs his mama."

She had the rifle pointed at Charlie. It would be a simple thing to slam it aside, dive for Abby, or turn the car sharply. Or …

Whatever Charlie did, she couldn't injure Abby or Charlie would never find the key.

It wasn't a very big key. She had noticed the keyring hanging on the nail in the garage yesterday when she had gone there looking for duct tape to seal up a box. There was also a house key on the chain, both keys attached to a dirty old rabbit's foot. Abby could have done anything with them. What if she'd just locked the door and then flung the keys as hard as she could out into the darkness? How would they ever find them in time? The clock was ticking.

Tick. Tick.

Merrie was in there in the dark.

Stop it!

Think.

The nearest place where the county line crossed the road was on Route 17 North. Barber's Mill Road connected to 17 about halfway between the county line and the Middle of Nowhere. As she recalled, there was not a Welcome to Nowhere County sign, just a simple state sign that said Entering Beaufort County. She had to be sure not to blow past that sign, so she slowed down.

The road curved to the left about fifty feet after the sign, where the Rolling Fork River snuggled up beside it on the right, rushing dark water flowing north back into Beaufort County. Every time the river flooded, which had been every spring of Charlie's life, traffic bound for Beaufort County was diverted to Route 17 North because the river banks were steep here, the river flowing by twenty or thirty feet below the level of the road.

She began to slow the car. She couldn't take a chance on blowing past the sign and wind up with Abby in the Dollar General Store parking lot, violently sick. The shape Abby was in, another trip through might kill her and then how would they ever find the key?

"Up there," Abby said, gesturing with her chin toward the Beaufort County sign, its iridescent lettering glowing in the headlights. "Stop there."

Charlie pulled off the road stopped and put the car in park.

Now that they were no longer moving, the headlights caught the shimmer of something in the road about fifty feet ahead, the shiny mirage, the face of the Jabberwock.

"Abby …"

"Get out."

"You can't shoot me. How will you get out if you kill me?"

"Ain't gonna kill you outright, just shoot your knees out, one at a time, then … This here's a .22. If I'm careful, I can shoot you a dozen times without killing you. That'll take a while, though, and yore little girl ain't got that kind of time."

Abby had it all figured out. She gestured with the gun barrel and Charlie opened the door and stepped out. She noticed the blood on the car seat where Abby had been sitting. It wasn't a whole lot of blood, but she'd been bleeding a small amount for a very long time. Her nose wasn't bleeding now, but red tears streamed down her cheeks. How long would it be before she passed out from the loss of blood?

"Go on now."

The river flowed by in the darkness off to the right. Charlie could hear it bubbling.

"You go on up there to that thing and do … do whatever it is you gotta do. Pull out that invisible sword you got, and cut off its head."

Charlie walked slowly toward the Jabberwock, trying to decide what to do. How to convince, or trick, or overpower or …

It occurred to Charlie then, for the first time, that she would die here, that she was living the last few minutes of her life. Abby would be furious when Charlie didn't, couldn't, make the monster go away. She might shoot her dead right here in the middle of the road. And if she did, Merrie would die, too.

No, Charlie had to think of … something.

Chapter Thirty-Two

Sam's heart leapt into her throat when they rounded the final bend and her headlights illuminated a car pulled off on the shoulder of the road on the river side and two figures standing in front of it in the spill of the headlights. Only two.

"Where's Merrie?" Sam wondered aloud.

"In the car, I guess. Asleep in the backseat or something. Look, are sure you want to do this?" Malachi asked.

"Yeah, I'm sure."

"Okay, then, just remember to stay out of my way. Approach her slowly and I'll do the same on the other side, so she can't keep the gun on both of us at the same time. But she'll try. She'll swing it back and forth. I'll catch her when she swings."

Sam nodded, her heart hammering in her ears so loud she hoped she'd heard all he said to her. She pulled her Taurus to a stop behind the Honda Legend belonging to Sam's mother. Charlie was standing in the middle of the road dressed in a terrycloth bathrobe, and a bloody, ragged Abby stood just off the asphalt in the dirt. Though she appeared barely able to stand, her grip on Malachi's rifle seemed firm and she had it pointed at Charlie.

Sam got out on the driver's side, hanging back. Stood there in the darkness, ridiculously aware of the chirping crickets, the honk of tree frogs and the damp smell of the reeds around the river. Malachi got out on the passenger side and walked directly toward the two figures in the road.

"What're you doin' here?" Abby cried. "You go on along and leave us be."

"She put Merrie in the kiln, locked her in there," Charlie cried, but that couldn't be right. Sam had misunderstood, hadn't heard right. Charlie couldn't possibly mean—

"That littlun's gonna stay there till she dies 'less you all go away. Leave now!"

Sam *hadn't* misunderstood! Oh, dear god …

"Abby, we just want to talk—

Abby leveled the rifle full at Malachi.

"I will shoot you down like a mad dog if you take one more step."

The level of rage, malice and total insanity was horrifying. Malachi stopped.

Showtime.

Sam called out to Abby from where she stood. Sam'd turned off the headlights of her car, so she was in shadow standing beside the driver's door.

"Abby, she doesn't have to kill the Jabberwock. You don't have to go to Lexington to get Cody. He's *here*."

She took another couple of steps to bring herself even with Charlie's car, but she was careful not to step out into the spill of the headlights.

Abby gasped, the gun faltered.

"What're you sayin' 'bout my Cody?"

Out of the corner of her eye, Sam saw Malachi move

toward Abby, but Abby quickly recovered, leveled the rifle at his chest.

"I guess you're tired of living, cause I'm gonna put a bullet—"

"Shep brought him," Sam interrupted. "Took him to your house but you weren't there. He asked me to take care of the baby while he looked for you. He's out right now, searching for you."

"*Shep?*"

Sam stepped up then, not into the spill of the lights but out from the shadows to beside the left front tire.

"Abby, don't you want to hold your baby?"

Sam cradled a baby-sized bundle in her arms, wrapped in the ratty afghan she always carried in her backseat. She nuzzled her face into the blanket and kissed the concealed face of the doll wrapped inside.

"Cody?"

The longing in Abby's voice would have broken Sam's heart if she weren't standing there about to shoot Malachi.

"The kiln's full of stuff — there's only a little air and Abby *hid* the key," Charlie cried. "Don't give her the baby until she tells me where the key is."

Even when Charlie spoke, Abby kept the gun pointed at Malachi. If she kept it trained on him, Sam would have to be the one to jump her. She could do it. Abby was a little bitty thing. Sam had six inches and thirty pounds on her.

"You bring me my boy!" Abby said.

"Don't!" Charlie said. "Not until she—"

"You shut up, witch," Abby cried. Her attention was focused on Charlie but the rifle was still aimed at Malachi. "All of this is your fault." To Sam, she said, "I want my Cody, you bring him on—"

"How're you going to hold a gun and Cody at the same time?" Malachi asked.

"He's hungry," Sam said. "Cody's got his little fist wrapped around my finger and he's sucking on the end of it. You need to nurse him."

She took the words like a blow, almost staggered forward.

"Where's the key?" Charlie demanded. "*No key, no baby!*"

"I got the key right here in my pocket." Abby ducked her chin and indicated the pocket on the front of the filthy, bloody, ragged Mickey Mouse smock from the Dollar Store. "Danglin' on that old rabbit's foot fob with that other little bitty key and that big ole door key that likely don't open nothing." There was a lump in the pocket. That was it, then. Now, they just had to get the gun away from her without anybody getting hurt.

"You bring him here right now."

Sam walked slowly, cutting her eyes to Malachi, who was maybe twenty feet away from Abby with the rifle aimed at his chest. Sam nodded to him almost imperceptibly.

Then Charlie started toward Abby.

"I said, no key, no baby," she said. "Give me the key!"

"No!" Abby backed up a step, started to turn the gun toward Charlie, but didn't, just told Sam, "I done told you once — give me my baby right now!" When Sam didn't move, Abby cocked her head to the side, almost sounded like a little kid. "You don't think I'm serious, do you? Guess I need to prove it."

She turned her attention back toward Malachi and put her eye to the sight on the rifle. Without a moment's hesitation, she shot him.

Chapter Thirty-Three

The sound of the gunshot shattered the cricket warmth of the night like a bomb. There was a heartbeat of silence then, before Malachi crumpled to the ground. Sam screamed and rushed to where he lay on his side on the road. She probably didn't even notice that she had dropped the bundle on the road.

Abby noticed!

Charlie watched horror wash over Abby's face when she thought Sam'd dropped her baby ... then saw the horror morph into rage when the doll rolled out of a ragged afghan onto the pavement. Abby turned, racking another shell into the chamber as she aimed the weapon at Sam. Charlie charged. She dived through the air, catching Abby around the midsection like a tackle going after a running back heading into the end zone. The rifle went off, the shot blasting out into the night as she landed on top of Abby, tried for a grip on the rifle but felt a bump, instead, not really painful, just stunning, a blow to the head like she'd stood up from leaning into the refrigerator and whacked her head on the freezer door she'd left open above her.

The world stopped being real for a heartbeat or two, while pain rushed to replace the numb spot on her temple and she felt herself tumbling onto her right side, her cheek scraping across the rough asphalt.

The whole thing couldn't have lasted more than a second or two, but that was all Abby'd needed. The rifle she'd slammed into the side of Charlie's head was now pinned between them. She let go of it, wiggled out from under Charlie's body and was gone.

Charlie came back to herself in time to see the bloody scrub shirt vanish out of the spill of headlights down the embankment toward the river. She staggered to her feet, only three or four strides behind Abby, and ran — dizzy — after her. At the edge of the road, she hit a wall of black. She'd been staring into the car headlights and the darkness beyond them was a wall of tar. She plunged forward anyway, lost her balance and fell forward and slid on her belly halfway down the riverbank, through bushes that caught on the terrycloth of her bathrobe and briars that grabbed at her hair and face.

It was totally dark — like the inside of the kiln! The thought froze Charlie's breath as she struggled to her feet, squinting into the black in front of her, trying to get her feet under her so she could keep going.

Staggering forward another couple of steps, she broke free of an oleander bush she'd tangled with and crossed a clear space two or three more steps. Her feet splashed into water. Any farther and she'd be in the river, and Abby was *in front of her,* which meant she already was.

"Charlie!" she heard Sam's voice calling from above her. "Charlie, are you down there?"

She looked back up the hill at the black silhouette

standing at the top of the ridge, light glowing all around her, then she turned her face back to the darkness of the river in front of her. She was too late. Abby was out there somewhere in the dark water and Charlie had absolutely no hope of finding her. Surely she'd already been washed downstream the thirty or forty feet to the Jabberwock. She was gone, and if Charlie wasn't careful, the current would carry her there, too. And she couldn't let herself be grabbed right now, land disoriented and desperately sick in a bus shelter. She had to get to Merrie. Had to get her out of that kiln.

And the woman with the key to the kiln in her pocket had just ridden the Jabberwock to the Dollar General Store parking lot in the Middle of Nowhere.

SAM HAD HEARD about people who froze, just suddenly couldn't move. But it had never happened to her until she heard the gunshot and turned to see Malachi Tackett grab his chest and crumple to the road.

She couldn't move. Froze as solid as a hood ornament.

Except she didn't.

While her mind was processing the fact that she was frozen, the rest of her body was obeying the messages she was sending. She screamed, heard herself make a sound like a scream. And the next thing she knew she was kneeling beside Malachi, seeing the blood on the back of his shirt and some part of her brain processing that and being glad about it.

She had no memory, no sense of movement, no spatial history in her muscles to explain how she could have been standing beside the car one instant and the next leaning over Malachi, with absolutely no passage of time in between.

As she turned him over from his side to his back she heard another gunshot, but that was out there where the world was doing its thing, but Sam Sheridan was all about and only about one thing. Malachi Tackett. She took hold of the halves of his button-down shirt and ripped downward, sending buttons pinging off like shrapnel into the night.

Abby'd had the gun trained on Malachi's chest. She'd fired at a range of only twenty feet. But either her aim was off or Malachi had started to move out of the way a fraction of a second before she pulled the trigger because when Sam lifted up his tee shirt she saw that the bullet wound was not in the *top* left quadrant of his chest. It was in the *lower* left quadrant a little higher than his navel and far out on the edge. That was the entry wound. There'd been an exit wound on his back that Sam'd seen and recorded the information for use later, which meant the bullet had entered his left side, cut a path through his body about two inches below the skin and exited out the back. It might have ricocheted off a rib in its progress through his body but she didn't think the angle was right for that. What else she didn't think was that the injury was life-threatening. A bullet wound in that spot could not have entered and exited through any vital organs. Though painful and bleeding like a spigot, it was what they called in all the cop movies "a flesh wound."

She ripped the front half of his shirt off from the shoulder seam, thinking as she did that it took a lot of strength to rip fabric like that, but it was another piece of information she filed for future perusal. She yanked the arm hole seam apart and pulled the piece of fabric down the side seam and off into her hand. Then she ripped the piece of cloth into two halves. She wadded up one piece and jammed it into the hole in his side on the front, deep into the hole, heard him groan but didn't care. Then she rolled him onto his side and did the same thing with the exit wound on his back.

Then she took a breath. Possibly the first one she'd taken since she knelt beside him, which had to have been less than a minute ago. Then she leapt up, raced to her car, yanked open the back passenger side door — please let it be here, please, oh please let it still be there! — and felt around in the dark footwell and under the front — *there!* The ACE bandage from the small plastic tub she used to carry supplies — stethoscope, thermometer, blood pressure cuff — while she was working had fallen out of the tub when she was unloading it on Friday afternoon, and she had meant to go back and get it.

She heard his voice as she was running back to kneel beside him, had probably been hearing it the whole time she'd been crouched there, but had not until now attended to the sound. Which, of course, was words and it took her a moment to shift her brain into the mode that translated words into meanings.

"... all right? Where is she?" he asked.

Charlie.

Sam's head snapped up and she saw the rifle lying on the roadside. Charlie and Abby were gone.

"... they went down toward the river," he said, his voice breathless from the pain.

She held the end of the ACE bandage to his abdomen and wrapped it once around his body to hold the wadded-up fabric bandages in place, then she shoved the remainder of the roll into his left hand and placed it over the piece of fabric in the wound in his side.

"Press here. Hard. Keep pressure on it and don't let go."

Then she got to her feet and ran past the rifle on the ground to the top of the embankment, calling out for Charlie.

A voice came up to her from the darkness below, along with the sound of somebody scrambling up through the bushes and over the rocks.

"… into the river," were the first discernible words, but the voice was Charlie's and that's what Sam had so desperately wanted to know. "I was right behind her and I hit the water. She had to have gone in." Charlie emerged from the dark bushes and raced toward Sam. Her pajama pants were muddy up almost to the knee. Her robe was untied and flapping around her.

A random thought rode a single synapse through her brain — Charlie's hair was perfect, looked just like Princess Diana — and then was gone.

"… Malachi hurt bad?"

Charlie brushed past her to Malachi, looked down at him, then back up at Sam.

"Abby went into the river so she must have washed downstream into the Jabberwock. She has the key to the kiln in her pocket. *I have to get that key.*"

Her voice got higher and more hysterical with every word. "Merrie's in the kiln. That monster put her in the kiln *and shut the door!*" She looked at her watch and squeaked out an aborted scream. "*It's three thirty-two. Merrie's only got enough air to last until three forty-five* — that's thirteen minutes and it takes *twenty minutes to drive*—" She cut herself off, cried out hysterically, *"No!"*

She clamped her jaw shut, ground her teeth, spoke with words wrapped in iron control.

"No, that's an hour and she has more time than that.

There's enough air for an hour *and a half.* There *is!* Until *4:15.*" Charlie was hanging onto her emotions with her fingernails, fighting hysteria. "Maybe longer, another …" She pulled in air and a sob rode with it. "I've got *forty-three minutes!* Merrie will die in—"

"Pull me up," Malachi spoke from below them and they looked down at him. He was trying to rise.

"Malachi, don't," Sam said. "You shouldn't—"

He grabbed Sam's restraining hand. His voice was gruff. "Pull me up!"

She pulled him up.

"Sam, you need to go to the bus shelter and get that key out of Abby's pocket and take it to Charlie's," Malachi said. Sam just looked at him, her understanding lagging a beat or two behind his words. "Go now!" He was standing now, bent in pain at the waist but holding the roll of ACE bandage in place. "Charlie and I'll go to her house and see if we can find some other way to get the door open." Sam only paused for a beat, was turning toward her car as he urged her to "Hurry."

She called over her shoulder as she ran, "Roll that bandage around and around *tight.*"

Then she was in her car, wheeling it around in the middle of the road like a Nascar driver and racing off into the darkness.

Chapter Thirty-Four

It was a good thing Malachi was doing the thinking because Charlie didn't seem to be able to. She was totally consumed by the monster imperative: *Get Merrie out of the kiln!* She could hear only that, banging around in her head, blotting out all other sound or thought.

After he instructed Sam to go to the bus shelter, he grabbed hold of her arm.

"Help me to your car."

She didn't question. Just wrapped his arm around her shoulder and helped him walk to her car.

When Sam wheeled her car around in a skidding turn and raced away into the night, the action freed Charlie from some kind of trance. Suddenly, she no longer felt like her thoughts were wrapped in cotton, her actions lagging behind her volition. She was absolutely here and now, totally present. Could smell the river on her clothes, was aware of the pebbly asphalt on the bottom of her bare feet and the weight of the man leaning against her.

She got the door open and helped Malachi inside. Then she bolted around the car and jumped into the driver's seat, started the car as Malachi began to wrap the ACE bandage around and around his abdomen. Then she turned the car around and pointed it back into Nowhere County and sped away into the worst hours of her entire life.

The drive from the county line down Route 17 to Barber's Mill Road, and then down that to her mother's house, took only seconds. Seconds that were hours long. Charlie was not aware of the passage of time or of driving the car or what Malachi was saying, and he was saying something.

She'd blinked when she got behind the wheel. And when she blinked again, she was careening into the driveway of her mother's house and it wasn't likely she'd ever remember anything about the time in between.

She slammed the transmission into park, leapt out of the car, leaving the door open and the engine running.

From the car to the back gate.

Through the back gate into the unlit backyard, where a hammer slammed into her chest. The kiln was a puddle of deeper darkness just beyond the side door of the garage, but even with only the light of the full moon, she could see it well enough to know that the door on it was closed.

She took one step and she was standing in front of it. She took one breath, then reached out and grabbed the cold metal handle and yanked on it with every ounce of strength in her body. It didn't move. The door wasn't just closed. It was locked.

Almost the whole backyard was dirt, her mother's unplanted vegetable garden. But there was a slice of grass beside the garage all the way to the gate that probably hadn't been mowed since ... You could see an indentation in the tall grass in front of the kiln where the door had been opened, had swung out across the grass and bent it down. In fact, several blades of grass had been caught in the door when it closed and were now stuck there.

She might have started sobbing then. She knew she was making some kind of sound, but she couldn't hear it.

There was a slab of concrete in front of the side garage door and a small roof jutting out from the building over it with an overhead light, though no sidewalk attached the side door of the garage to the screened-in porch on the back of the house.

She flung open the garage door and slammed her hand on the light switch on the inside wall beside it and stepped inside. The dim florescent in the ceiling flickered a time or two, then remained on. It cast a paltry glow through the big dusty-smelling enclosure, but it was enough light to see the ten-penny nail in the wall behind the door.

The nail was bare.

Some part of her mind registered that it was only recently bare, too. She'd noted when she'd gone looking for duct tape to seal up boxes that the garage was so coated with dusty cobwebs she'd need a face mask if she moved anything or the dust would ignite a brushfire in her allergies.

The rest of the garage was still enshrouded in cobwebs. But there were no cobwebs around that nail now.

She gasped a strangled sob, her hands flew to her mouth and she actually staggered backward a step.

Oh, dear God in heaven *it was true.*

This was real.

Somehow on the drive from the county line that never happened, she had managed to convince herself it was a bluff. Abby hadn't really *locked* a three-year-old child in an airless kiln and stolen the *only key.* Nobody was that kind of monster.

She'd put the child in the kiln, laid her on the piece of

Mama's new carpet, but left the door open a crack, just enough to let in air.

Or she had closed the door, but left it unlocked.

Or she'd locked it, but put the key back on the nail.

Reality was a thing too hateful to countenance. Abby Clayton hadn't been bluffing. She had done *exactly* what she'd said. She'd used the key on the nail to unlock the kiln and opened the door — you could see the impression in the grass. She'd *seen how full it was*, that there was barely any room ... but still she had put Merrie inside, closed and locked the door and dropped the key — the one "danglin' on that old rabbit's foot fob with that other little bitty key and the big ole door key that likely don't open nothing" into her pocket.

Now Abby was gone. And the key in her pocket was the only way to open the kiln.

Charlie looked at her watch. Three fifty-six. Nineteen minutes.

SAM WENT roaring into the parking lot of the Dollar General Store so fast if any of the handful of people there had been in her way, she'd have run them down.

The lights the fire department had set up were still turned on, bleaching the color out of the world. She threw the car into park and leapt out, her head on a swivel, her eyes searching. Liam Montgomery was there. He must have gone home and changed out of his uniform because he was wearing street clothes now. When she ran across the lot to the bus shelter he followed her there.

"What's goin'—?"

No way to tell him now. No time.

"Where's Abby?"

"Abby Clayton?"

"Of course, Abby Clayton. Where is she?"

"I don't know. She's not here."

The words punched a hole in Sam's belly, the blow almost physical.

"Not here?"

"She was here earlier. You know that. After you took Charlie home, you came back and—"

"Not then. I'm not talking about then. Where is she *now*?"

Sam raced out into the center of the lot, looking for something that had no place to hide. The asphalt was still wet. Somebody'd been hosing it down because there was no smell of any kind now. Roscoe Tungate and his brother Harry were still here.

Harry Tungate approached her.

"You find her?" he asked. "You find Abby?"

"No, she's *here* somewhere." That was irrational, because it was clear Abby Clayton was not there. "She has to be."

"Why do you think she's—?"

"She went through the Jabberwock twenty minutes ago."

It might not even have been that long. Sam had *flown* down Route 17 from the county line to the Middle of Nowhere. Without having to turn off on Barber's Mill Road, that wound its slow way through the hollow to Charlie's mother's house at the base of Little Bear Mountain, it was a straight shot.

The Jabberwock should have deposited Abby here long before …

But had Abby actually gone through the Jabberwock? Charlie had said she was in the river. The current would have washed her downstream and it was only about thirty, maybe forty feet to the Jabberwock. But had she somehow avoided it? Had she …

Sam was grasping at straws.

… hidden in the bushes in the darkness and Charlie hadn't seen her?

Or did she somehow swim *against* the current? The river was narrow and deep there, the curve had washed away the outside edge, making a hole a little past the Jabberwock so deep kids sometimes went there to go swimming. The water at the river's edge was only about a foot deep, but would have been three or four feet deep within a few feet from the shore. Had Abby somehow managed to fight that current, in the dark, and swim *up*stream?

Why would she do that?

What she wanted — all she wanted — was in the opposite direction. Abby wanted to get out of the county, go get her baby. It'd make no sense for her to swim the other way.

But clearly she had gone *somewhere* because she wasn't here.

Sam hadn't been allowing herself to consider the ramifications of that, but she did now and the reality slammed like a wrecking ball into her chest.

Without the key in Abby's pocket, Charlie's little girl would die.

Chapter Thirty-Five

Charlie didn't know how much time she had spent banging her fists on the closed kiln door and screaming before Malachi took her by the shoulders and pulled her away. When he did, she turned into his arms and sobbed, great heaving, wrenching sobs that rose from the core of her being and tore her open as they exploded out of her.

Her baby was locked up in there. In that tomb, that stone sarcophagus. There was no air in the tomb and without air, her baby would die.

She found herself screaming again at the thought, but Malachi just held her while she did, held her when her knees folded up beneath her and she sank to the ground and he eased himself down beside her and put his arm around her shoulders.

Then her head snapped up.

She looked at her watch.

"It's 4:01. Sam's at the bus shelter by now, surely. It takes less than twenty minutes to get from the county line to the Middle of Nowhere."

"I'm sure she's been there and gone by now."

"On her way here — right! How long can it take to get a key out of a pocket?"

"If she's driving anything like the way she drove when I was with her, she'll come skidding into that driveway any second now."

"Any second." Charlie looked at her watch again. "Yeah, any second."

She held onto the hope in those words, clinging to that tiny piece of driftwood in a hurricane-tossed sea.

"And there's still fourteen minutes — and maybe more. We don't know for sure." Charlie recited aloud the math she'd been figuring and refiguring in her head again and again. Length times width times height divided by twenty-seven … Abby'd said by thirty, but Charlie used twenty-seven. Six feet by six feet by six feet was 216 square feet, divided by twenty-seven was eight. *Empty*, there was almost eight cubic yards of air inside the kiln. Merrie could sleep peacefully in there all night. But the kiln wasn't empty; it was almost full — of *stuff*. Boxes of pots, cups, bowls, vases, ashtrays — pottery. There were sacks of powdered clay, boxes of tools, a potter's wheel, *Christmas decorations* — maybe the artificial tree, too. And a stack of carpet rolls! All that stuff was taking up space, reducing the amount of air inside the kiln, air Merrie needed to breathe.

Charlie looked at her watch again. How could five minutes have passed? It wasn't a digital watch and she could almost see the hands spinning around and around, faster and faster and—

Less than ten minutes.

"Could we pick the lock?" She said the words as she was thinking them, then scrambled to her feet, buoyed up by the hope that had swelled inside her like pulling the cord on a Navy dinghy. "We *could!* How? How do you pick a lock? But it can be done. You can use … what do you use? Something small, a piece of wire."

She knew she was babbling and could tell from the look on Malachi's face that he didn't for a moment believe it would work. But it would. He'd see. They'd pick the lock and get the door open before Sam even got here with the key.

"I'll find some wire to use."

She turned and ran into the garage, looking at everything at the same time, which amounted to looking at nothing at all. She had to focus, but there was precious little to focus on. Unlike the basement that she'd glanced into last night, the garage wasn't filled with leftover *whatever,* the flotsam and jetsam of a life that her mother didn't need anymore. The rows of shelving that once held pottery were now weighed down, stacked three and four deep, with hundreds of Mason jars where her mother had canned the vegetables she grew in her garden. The best of the pottery that'd once sat there was stored now in boxes in the kiln!

The workbench didn't have tools on it. A couple of flower pots sat on the far end. Some plastic vases from the flowers she or her sister sent to their mother on Mother's Day took up dusty residence beside a small bag of plant food, two rusty buckets and a washtub. There was nothing in the garage smaller than a screwdriver. There was no hammer of any kind, any size.

The space where her mother once had conducted ceramics classes was empty, the tables and benches gone. A wheelbarrow with a flat tire leaned up against the wall resting on its handles. Garden implements — rakes, hoes, shears, hand spades and an ancient pair of cotton gloves — hung from nails on the wall. There were bicycle racks where she and her sister must have kept their bikes but she had no memory of that. The big bay door was shut. If she needed more light she could pull it up. She'd left the car headlights on, but more light wouldn't help her find what wasn't there.

She turned around and headed back outside, on her way to the kitchen to search the house for—

"I don't think trying to pick the lock is a good idea," Malachi said, and some small part of her registered that he was bent over slightly, using his left elbow to press on the top of the bandage in the bullet wound in his side. Bullet wound. *Abby'd shot him!*

Then the thought and concern were gone.

"Why not?"

"Because we could damage the lock, digging around inside it with the wrong tools, no clue what we're doing. We could bend something, scratch something, knock something out of place so when Sam gets here with the key, it won't work."

He was absolutely right, of course. What was she thinking? They didn't dare fool with the lock.

Charlie looked at her watch and wanted to scream. It was like some cartoon watch where the second and minute hands spun around and around, trailing the hour hand along with them. It was 4:10. Five minutes left.

"I did the math in my head, but maybe I did it wrong. My mind's too ... help me figure ..."

She didn't have to tell him what math. He'd grown up around coal mining same as she had. He looked at the building.

"Six feet square ... that's six by six ..."

He continued to figure. Came up with the same numbers she had — eight hours if it were empty.

"But it's not empty."

"What's in—?"

"Stuff. Junk. Boxes. Storage. I haven't looked in it in years."

"How much stuff? How much space was left?"

And that was the thing. As she recalled, the kiln had been ... *almost full* of boxes.

Bang, her mind backed up from that thought so fast she tripped mentally, stumbled. No, she was wrong. That wasn't it. There was almost nothing in the kiln. It was ... almost empty. And empty, there *were eight hours of air.*

It's not empty. The voice spoke in her ear but Charlie wouldn't listen.

"There was no spare key," she said, answering the question Malachi hadn't asked. "Just the one. And Mama almost never locked the thing, just fastened it shut when she was firing something. She only locked it when she stopped using it ... to make sure no kid got trapped ..."

Reality again dumped a ton of rocks on her head.

"Malachi, my baby's *in there!*"

She turned to the kiln and hammered her fists on the door.

The phone in the house rang.

Who could possibly be calling at this hour? She didn't even turn toward it.

"Maybe it's Sam, and she ..." He stopped, obviously sorry he'd said anything at all.

Her knees again turned to bags of water. If Sam had the key, she'd be on her way here with it. The only reason she'd have to call was if she *didn't* have the key.

Charlie looked helplessly into Malachi's eyes. She *couldn't* ... she absolutely could not answer that—

"I'll get it." He began hobbling across the grass toward the back porch steps. She could see that his wounds were bleeding again, had soaked through the ACE bandage. She ought to care about that but there was nothing left inside her to care with …

She placed her lips close to the not-crack where the door fit so tight you couldn't have slid a piece of paper between it and the jamb.

"We're coming, sweetheart. Mommy's coming. It won't be long."

Then she was sitting beside the door, leaning against it, didn't remember sitting down. She was speaking into the crack but she didn't know what she was saying.

Merrie'd been a bumblebee last Halloween. She'd been adorable in the costume, yellow and black stripes and tiny bumblebee wings. It even had a rubber stinger on the butt and a little hat with antennae on coiled wires.

Charlie had gone trick-or-treating with her, of course, held her hand, walked her up the sidewalks to each house in the neighborhood. She helped Merrie hold out the sack for the candy. Some of the neighbors had dressed up. Her friend Laverne came to the door as the Wicked Witch of the West and Merrie'd cowered away from her until she popped the fake wart off her nose and lifted the hat with long, stringy black hair attached so Merrie could see her blonde curls underneath.

Charlie didn't let Merrie keep any of the candy, of course. She had an identical Halloween sack full of candy hidden in the pantry, so she could swap it out and Merrie would never know. She wasn't about to let the child eat candy that'd been given to her by a stranger!

That was dangerous. No telling what—

Merrie was behind these stone walls in an airless room. If she didn't get out soon …

Merrie would die. The most horrible words in the English language. No, not the most horrible. The most horrible were only three words, too. Merrie's already dead.

When she saw the look on Malachi's face, she didn't even have to ask.

She heard his words — "Abby's not there" — and the world went dark. Charlie McClintock left the building.

Chapter Thirty-Six

Sam drove slowly through the night toward Charlie's house with no urgency and no hope. She had *flown* down Route 17 to the Middle of Nowhere, looking at her watch every few seconds. If Abby'd been there when Sam arrived in the Dollar Store parking lot, Sam would have snatched the key out of her pocket and raced to Charlie's. She'd have made it there by ten minutes after four, with time to spare. They'd have used the key to open the kiln while Merrie still had air to breathe.

But Abby hadn't been there.

As the minutes of Merrie's life ticked away, Sam had paced around the empty parking lot searching, like she'd suddenly stumble over Abby's body and she just hadn't noticed it before.

Sam had waited. And waited. Considering and discarding ways to save the child without the key.

They could ... drill a hole in the kiln to let in air.

The walls were solid stone a foot thick with interior ceramic plates two inches thick. Where could they find a drill with a masonry bit that long? And there was no time to look.

Break into the kiln, then use a sledgehammer and a chisel … Would Charlie's mother have a sledgehammer? Chisels? How long would it take to dig through solid rock?

Longer than ten minutes.

And after a while … they didn't even have ten minutes.

Sam pulled in behind Charlie's mother's car in the driveway, turned off the key and sat for a moment. Gathered herself. The others in the parking lot had been horrified by her story. Liam, Abner, Rodney and the Tungate brothers wanted to dash to Charlie's house to … yeah, to what? Break into the kiln? Even if they could have done that — and they couldn't — by the time they were even considering it, it was too late. Some had wanted to come to Charlie's with Sam — E.J. and Liam and Thelma Jackson — to … Again, to what? Just be there. But Sam'd told them no, that Charlie didn't need an audience.

What Sam was about to see was unfathomable grief and horror. Malachi had told her on the phone that Charlie was only a shade this side of completely hysterical and Sam was sure when Malachi told her Abby wasn't at the bus shelter …

Sam refused to put herself in Charlie's shoes, to imagine what it would be like if it were Rusty locked in an airless kiln. Dying in there. *Dead* in there. She had resolutely shoved those horror nightmares out of her mind, but when she picked him up at Damien's house, whenever that was … she would hug the boy harder than he ever allowed himself to be hugged. She'd kiss his whole face and not care that a twelve-year-old boy did not allow his mother to kiss him. She'd do it anyway. Right there in front of his friend. She didn't care.

After she got out of the car, she reached back in and

got the bundle of gauze, sterile pads and tape she had brought to re-bandage Malachi's wounds. As she walked toward the back gate leading into the backyard, she noticed it was dawn. Dawn out there on the flat anyway. A new day that wouldn't officially arrive here in the mountains until the sun cleared the crest of Chisolm Bluff, the tallest mountain to the east, in about an hour and a half. But the sky above was blue, not black. The stars and the moon were gone. Light spilled over the top of the mountain and cascaded into the hollow below to give a golden glow to everything, brighten the puddles of shadows until they melted away and it was day.

She opened the gate. The light above the side door of the garage shined down on Charlie and Malachi but the growing daylight gave texture to the rest of the yard, too. Charlie sat on the ground beside the door of the kiln, appeared to be talking into the crack.

As Sam got closer, she could hear that Charlie was singing.

"... gonna buy you a mockingbird. And if that mockingbird don't sing, mama's gonna buy you a diamond ring."

The lump formed so instantly in Sam's throat tears literally squirted out of her eyes and down her cheeks. Malachi was on his knees behind Charlie, his hands on her shoulders, looked like he'd been rubbing her back. Sam knew Charlie had no idea he was there. She had gone to a whole other world, another dimension of human misery where there was no light or tenderness or hope.

Sam hadn't wanted to think about it as she drove to the house, but as she stood now looking at the stone monolith beside Charlie's garage, she couldn't imagine how they would *ever* get the door of the kiln open until they could find Abby and get the key. Liam said he and the Tungate brothers were going down to search the riverbank as soon as it got light. Sam thought that, given the shape Abby was in, she might have finally bled out or been too weak to swim and she'd drowned and her body was lying …. Yeah, lying *where?* If her dead body had washed down through the Jabberwock, wouldn't it have come out in the parking lot? Maybe you had to be alive to … If her body just washed on downstream, as long as the Jabberwock held the county hostage, there was no way to get to it.

And if they never found the key — never found Abby or found her body but the key wasn't in her pocket — how would they *ever* get the kiln open? Maybe Lester Peetree who used to run the hardware store in Twig would be able to … he wasn't a locksmith, though. It would take a lock-smith from Lexington or Louisville to get into the lock. And the Jabberwock …

Surely with enough manpower using jackhammers or chisels, there was some way to chisel into the bricks, dismantle the building from the outside. Or simply big men wielding sledgehammers — *bam, bam, bam* — destroy the building. Somehow, eventually, they'd get it open.

Malachi looked up when she approached. Charlie just kept singing. Sam noticed Charlie's hands, that her perfectly manicured nails were broken off, her fingertips raw. How had … Then she saw a broken piece of finger-nail in the crack between the kiln door and the jamb.

Sam swallowed hard, gritted her teeth to choke off a sob. She tried to take in a deep breath but her diaphragm refused to expand, only allowed her little sips of air. She stood where she was, getting control of herself before she dropped to her knees on the ground beside the other two and told Malachi quietly, "I need to take a look at those bandages."

"Later."

"*Now.* What good are you to anybody if you pass out from blood loss?"

That convinced him, he relented and moved away from Charlie, who hadn't known he was there in the first place and didn't miss him when he was gone. He remained on his knees, which allowed Sam access to both the entrance and exit wounds. Though the wounds had continued to ooze, eventually soaking her makeshift bandages, the ACE bandage and his tee shirt, the bleeding appeared to be stopped now. She didn't remove what she'd stuffed into the bullet holes — that would start the bleeding again. She just unwound the ACE bandage, covered her makeshift bandages with gauze pads, then wrapped strips of gauze around and around his body to hold the bandages in place and taped the gauze down.

"I need to get you to E.J.'s and clean these. It'd be a mess if they get infected. Maybe put in a couple of stitches, too."

But she was speaking softly and Malachi was only half-listening. Both of them were concentrated on the woman whose grief pulsed off her like heat off a potbelly stove. They would remain with her until … well, for however long she needed them. Sam didn't know what would happen now, didn't know what should happen … what was the next step after a thing like this? So she just sat with Malachi while Charlie sang.

Chapter Thirty-Seven

Something like waves of consciousness washed over Charlie, periods when everything was grayed out, indistinct and unreal. Then she would snap awake. Aware.

And in awareness was the reality that her little girl was gone. Merrie was dead. That reality stood hot and stinking in front of her when she embraced awareness and the pain of it made it hard to breathe.

Charlie would die here, too. She knew she would cease to be alive in some real, tangible way because living, breathing, feeling the warmth of the sun on her skin while her baby daughter had died ... had *suffocated* ... was both a physical and a spiritual impossibility.

Merrie had been asleep. She'd just never awakened. That's what the coal miners said, the ones who contemplated the possibility of suffocation every time they "went down." As ways of dying went, suffocating was an easy way to go, they said. It wasn't painful. You just finally closed your eyes and didn't open them again.

Merrie had known nothing. Had just closed her eyes ... when was the last time Charlie had looked into those eyes?

She didn't know. Couldn't remember. And suddenly that thought was beyond too horrible to bear. *Couldn't remember?* She'd checked on Merrie-the-Veterinary-Assistant-in-Training often as the nightmare day wore on, but when she'd gone in the last time, Merrie was already crashed on the couch and was sound asleep when she lifted her into her arms to carry her to the car.

So the time before that. The last time she'd checked on her ...

Charlie didn't know. Didn't know the last words she'd said, either. Surely, it was *I love you.* She always said that, told Merrie that all the time. I love you. Surely she'd said ...

She realized that she was singing. "... diamond ring gets broke, Mama's gonna buy you a billy goat." Why was she singing *that?* She didn't even like the song, had never sung it to Merrie. She sang her little girl fun songs. Happy songs.

It suddenly seemed very important to get this right, to sing the right song, not some random melody the child had never heard before. It was important that Merrie recognize the song. How could she be comforted by it if she'd never heard it before?

"Puff the Magic Dragon lived by the sea. And frolicked in the autumn mist ..."

MERRIE in her Betty Boop nightgown, smelling sweet from the bath, is snuggled up close to her. She kisses the little girl's nose and continues the song. "... in a land called—"

SUDDENLY, the pain of loss and grief were so great they exploded out of Charlie's soul into the world. She leaned her head back, closed her eyes and screamed, *"Meeerrrrrie!"* Shrieked the word. *Wailed* it. The sound was so harsh and loud it tore her vocal cords in its ferocity.

A hushed silence followed.

A bird in the mulberry tree sang out a three-note melody.

Another bird in the sycamore tree replied.

And a voice spoke from the screened-in porch.

"Mommy, why are you yelling? Are you mad at me?"

Chapter Thirty-Eight

It was a dream, a fantasy, a hallucination. Even as Charlie swung her head toward the porch she knew there'd be nobody there, that she was just imagining—

Merrie stood on the top step of the porch. She was dressed, wearing a plain white tee shirt and cheap denim shorts, the outfit Charlie put on her to replace the Whitney Houston tee shirt and jeans Charlie had thrown away.

She was barefoot. Her hair was a tangle of curls in her eyes.

"Merrie."

Charlie said the word the way the proctor says a word at a spelling bee. Each of the syllables was pronounced properly but with no intonation or inflection of any kind. Just the word.

Sam choked out some kind of sound and only then, when Charlie glanced at Sam and Malachi — their faces shocked, stunned and delighted — *only then* did she even consider the possibility that what she was seeing was real.

"Merrie?" The name was a question then and the little

girl had begun to pick up on a strange vibe and didn't like it. "Where have you been?"

Someone asked the question with Charlie's voice and out her mouth but Charlie was incapable of speech.

"I waked up unner the bed. I don't 'member falling out. Then I couldna find you—"

Charlie shrieked then, a wail of utter joy, stumbled to her feet and raced to the back porch, snatching the child up into her arms sobbing.

Merrie, the little drama queen, tuned up and started crying, too.

How long that part lasted, Charlie didn't know.

She understood that she was upsetting the child with her hysterical delight, knew Merrie was confused and frightened. Fine. Charlie didn't care. The child would get over it. Or she wouldn't. Maybe she'd carry with her for the rest of her life the trauma of the morning she'd awakened under her bed, and walked out into the backyard of her grandmother's house to find her mother contemplating suicide. That was fine, too. Life did that to people. Experiences marked them, sometimes permanently. Much as she'd like to, Charlie couldn't protect her little girl from the vagaries and vicissitudes of life and if she were going to be marked by something, this day, this experience, this whole new world was certainly worthy of permanent psychological damage.

Sam and Malachi hung back, each wearing looks of such profound happiness she registered them in some permanent memory cells. She would look back at their faces, again and again, and know that those two people had been with her, had *stuck by her,* had gotten her through the single worst day of her life and someday she'd thank them for it.

But not today.

Chapter Thirty-Nine

Things didn't turn out like this.

Mothers didn't miraculously get their children back, alive and unharmed.

Little girls didn't bump up against bull-moose insanity and live to tell about it.

In the world of Malachi Tackett, mothers and their babies died. Horrible deaths. Every time. They were hacked apart by their neighbors or butchered by strangers. By the hundreds, the thousands, the tens of thousands.

There was never, *never* a happy ending.

But not this time.

This time, good had won. Evil had lost.

And even though it was just the one, the one against thousands, hundreds of thousands, this mother and this little girl had made it through the valley of the shadow of death and Malachi had been an eyewitness to every second of it.

This *mattered.* What was happening here in Charlie's kitchen while Sam made coffee and fussed over his bandages and Charlie could not stop touching her little girl and the adorable child was all giggles and cheeriness, shifted something fundamental in Malachi. He turned some kind of corner. He couldn't have articulated it and wouldn't try because to explain or quantify it was to diminish the power of it. He had been walking so very, very long in the darkness that the light of joy and hope made him squint.

The private war of Lance Corporal Malachi Tackett and the horror of Rwanda was by no means over. But this pivotal, seminal moment was a battle won, was at least the end of the beginning.

"… grinning your gums dry, Malachi," said Sam and he realized that the smile on his face was there because it had chosen to appear there not because it had been summoned as an act of will. "Smiles look good on you."

Merrie was sitting in her mother's lap, which Malachi would bet wasn't where she normally sat for breakfast. She dropped a dollop of grape jelly on her plate from the spoon where she was gleefully digging it out of the jar. He was reasonably certain her mother didn't allow the child to do something that messy and sticky, either, and Merrie seemed to be aware that she was in a no-harm, no-foul zone for the moment and she best make hay while she had the chance.

Merrie picked up the glob with her fingers and stuffed it into her sticky mouth. Nobody cared.

"Stop dawdling over the toast," Sam told him. "You promised to let me take you to E.J.'s and disinfect those holes in your belly. Do you think if you put it off long enough I'll forget? Putting it off isn't going to make it hurt any less."

And it did hurt! Oh, my yes it did, not that Malachi let on. He'd been shot before — had the scars to prove it —

and as bullet wounds went, this one was unspectacular. But it still *hurt!* He'd lost a lot of blood, too, felt weak and light-headed. Get shot in a war and medical care was only a chopper ride away. Here, not so much. He likely needed a transfusion and *that* wasn't going to happen.

They were all doing a pretty convincing dance around the gigantic elephant in the middle of the room, the reality of their lives and the bizarre occurrences of the past twenty-four hours. There was, after all, always the possibility that the world had righted itself during the night, that sanity and order and the normal functioning of the universe had returned to Nowhere County. That driving down Route 17 through the county line would be of no more consequence than it had been any one of the hundreds, thousands of times Malachi had done it before.

He didn't think so, but he suspected he was alone in that assessment. The women wanted to believe normal had blown back in on the heels of the storm he didn't believe had blown abnormal into their lives in the first place. They wanted to think the Middle of Nowhere would sink back into obscurity today and folks passing it would recall the bizarre happenings there in June of 1995 and comment about how so many people had been bamboozled by some cosmic practical joke, or had been victims of a mass group hallucination.

Folks would drive past the bus shelter and pay it no mind. Just drive away from the Middle of Nowhere and out into the rest of the world.

Oh, how he hoped that was so, how he wished it would be true. But he didn't for a New York minute believe it.

Charlie had insisted on going back to the Middle of Nowhere with Sam and Malachi. She had her reasons, he supposed, but he didn't know what they were and wouldn't likely have understood them if he had. If he were Charlie

McClintock, he couldn't have been dragged to that half acre of the planet by a team of Clydesdales and the Budweiser Beer wagon.

Or maybe he would. He was aware of, and would bet the others were feeling the same thing, that they were involved in something "other." Something "outside." And a thing like that wasn't a thing you just ignored, turned your back on and walked away.

It wasn't until they were in Sam's car on their way to the Dollar General Store that the elephant in the room lifted its trunk and blared out a tremendous honk.

"What do you think happened with Abby?" Sam asked Malachi.

Sam was driving. Malachi was in the front seat and Charlie and Merrie were behind. The people at the bus shelter knew what had happened at the county line — about Abby and the key. If Abby had shown up there, E.J. or Liam or Pete would have come dashing to Charlie's house with it even though it was too late. Nobody'd come. When Sam called E.J.'s office to give the others the news about Merrie half an hour ago, Abby still hadn't shown up.

"*With* Abby or *to* Abby?" Charlie wanted to know.

"You mean, why didn't she actually put Merrie in the kiln?" Malachi asked. "I'd like to think the whole thing was a bluff, that she was too decent a human being to lock a little girl up in a kiln." Malachi had picked up on the edge in Charlie's voice and he didn't begrudge her a single hard feeling. "But it's equally possible Abby *couldn't* do it. There are a lot of ways it could have played out."

He'd thought about it. They all had. Maybe Abby had planned to put the child in the kiln but thought it was empty. When she saw how full it was, she knew the child wouldn't have enough air. Or maybe she didn't care how full it was, but when she picked the child up, she realized she wouldn't have the strength to carry her all that way — out of the bedroom, down the hall, across the kitchen, the porch and the backyard. So she'd settled for sliding her under the bed. Behind the poufy ballerina bed skirt, the child was invisible.

"The 'too decent a human being' description begs the question: how'd she turn on Malachi and just *shoot* him?" Sam asked.

"She was crazy, had a stroke, wasn't in her right mind, wasn't responsible for her behavior ..." Charlie ticked off the phrases. "Any or all of that is supposed to buy her out of everything." Charlie paused, and her voice was full of the emotion she was concealing from the little girl beside her. "I'm working on that, but I am here to testify that I am *not* there yet."

"Malachi's lucky her aim was off," Sam said.

"It wasn't off."

Both women looked at him.

"The *sight's* not zeroed. It's off, low and to the right. You have to aim high left to hit center. She was aiming at my heart and if the bullet had gone where she intended it to go ... she'd have killed me."

They let that settle before Sam picked up the ball and began dribbling down the court again.

"Then what happened *to* her?"

"I think she's dead ... somewhere," Charlie said.

"Where?" Sam asked.

Malachi said nothing, just looked out the window.

Sam ran with it. "Okay, the possibilities are: She drowned and her body washed downstream. Or she swam upstream and got out of the river and ... went somewhere. For some reason."

"Or she went into the Jabberwock and never came out."

The silence that followed Malachi's words was as heavy as a down comforter.

"You think somebody could just *stay* …?" Sam asked.

"Sam's the only one we know for sure," Charlie said. "We know exactly when she went in and know she popped right out the other side. Like instantly."

"I was too busy throwing up to time it, but … yeah, pretty much instantly."

"The rest of us, though … how long were *we* … in there?" Malachi said.

"Remember now, we decided we're going to think positively," Sam chirped, relentlessly cheery. "Life's back to normal. I can pick up my dry cleaning in Carlisle. You can catch that plane back to …"

Maybe she didn't finish because she didn't know where. But it was more likely that it had occurred to her, as it had to Malachi, that they weren't going to leave here the same people they'd been. Back out there in the normal world … they'd be different. They'd changed. They'd made connections to each other. No, they'd made *re*-connections to each other. Involuntary or not, those connections were real. And strong.

"You guys do realize, don't you, that this is the first time all three of us have been in Nower County at the same time since the night of graduation," Charlie said.

Malachi did realize that. Did indeed. Had been thinking about it. Turning it over and over in his mind. Considering what possible significance there could be to … Maybe the others had, too, because nobody said anything after that. They rode the last mile to the parking lot in silence.

When Sam pulled to a stop in front of the Dollar

General Store, what they saw dashed their hopes for normal and ordinary. Thelma Jackson and Rodney Sentry had gone home, Pete Rutherford had returned and the Tungate brothers and Abner Riley had never left. Liam and Hank Bayless were loading a *body* into the back of Hank's pickup truck.

"We lost one," Pete said simply when they approached him. Hank got into his truck and Liam got in with him and they drove away. "Willie Cochran — you remember him, got his thumbs mashed off in the mine by a scoop when he was a kid."

Malachi remembered him.

"He's what — eighty-five, ninety years old?" Charlie said.

"*Was* eighty-seven. He showed up like Fish did, choking like he'd swallowed his tongue. But 'fore anybody could do anything for him, he just went limp. Heart attack, I suppose."

"He had heart problems," Sam said.

Malachi looked after where Hank's truck had disappeared around a bend.

"Where's he taking the body?"

There was no longer a funeral home in Nowhere County, but the facility remained. Somebody'd bought the Bascum's Mortuary building while Malachi was deployed, tried to turn the plush viewing rooms into a dress boutique. The business had failed, but Malachi figured the basement embalming parlor hadn't been part of the renovation, that there were still "body drawers" there that slid out of the wall.

"If the refrigeration system still works at Bascum's … but if not, Roscoe gave him the key to Foodtown." There was a beat of silence. "It has a walk-in freezer."

Sam shooed Malachi into E.J.'s office, where she could

do a professional job on his bandage. Merrie accompanied her because the little girl was, after all, the veterinarian's assistant. Charlie wandered from one of the "front line" people to the next, asking how things had been.

Business had been slow. But the conduit was definitely open.

Chapter Forty

When Liam Montgomery returned from Bascum's, he took out a pad and pencil and started taking notes and giving directions, standing in the shade beneath the awning of E.J.'s office. He'd stepped up to the plate admirably, given that he had no training and absolutely no idea what he was doing. Sam was impressed. He'd taken charge and would keep the wheels on until …

Until whenever.

Short term, until Senior Deputy Skeet Phillips sobered up and showed up and nobody was looking forward to *that*.

Long term … Nobody wanted to think long term.

Charlie had just come out of E.J.'s office with Merrie, who was pitching a fit because she wanted to stay and play with the bunnies, when Abner Riley let out a strangled cry. All eyes snapped to where he was standing. He was in front of the bus shelter and someone had just appeared there.

Someone. Or some*thing.*

Charlie turned and shoved Merrie back into Raylynn Bennett's arms and slammed the office door in their faces while Sam and Malachi started across the parking lot.

It was Abby and there was no way to tell if she was dead or alive. She looked dead. Long dead. Long dead and …

Her whole body was swollen like a corpse bloats when it decomposes. Sam had seen only one decomposing corpse in her life and the smell of it … Abby had no dead body stink. She just looked like a balloon was swelled up inside her.

Her face was a horror, totally unrecognizable. Nobody would have known who she was without the blonde hair and the telltale Mickey Mouse smock. It had been so baggy it had hung off her skinny frame and now it strained at the seams to contain her.

Sam outdistanced the others hurrying across the lot to help Abby, but when she got about fifteen feet away from the shelter, Malachi caught up and grabbed her arm. Wouldn't let her go any farther.

"Malachi," Sam began. "I need to—"

And that's when it happened.

Abby Clayton exploded.

It was as if a bomb had gone off inside her. Her head blew apart like a pumpkin dropped off the first-floor balcony onto the porch. The rest of her exploded as well, but her clothing prevented the spewing of body parts everywhere.

But her head …

Abby Clayton's head was all over the parking lot.

Charlie had caught up with Sam and Malachi, her eyes as big as marbles, her face the color of a new gym sock. She looked at Sam and opened her mouth, but had to find a breath before she could speak.

"What could *possibly* … what could cause a thing like that?"

There was no *medical* … but Sam knew. They all did.

"The Jabberwock," she heard herself say, her voice faint and airless.

Malachi's deep baritone was a whisper, too.

"With jaws that bite and claws that catch."

The End

A Note from the Author

Thank you for reading *The Jabberwock*.

If you enjoyed this book, you please consider writing a review on your favorite bookselling site so other readers might enjoy it too. Just a couple of sentences would mean a lot to me.

Thank you!

Ninie Hammon

About the Author

Ninie Hammon (rhymes with shiny, not skinny) grew up in Muleshoe, Texas, got a BA in English and theatre from Texas Tech University and snagged a job as a newspaper reporter. She didn't know a thing about journalism, but her editor said if she could write he could teach her the rest of it and if she couldn't write the rest of it didn't matter. She hung in there for a 25-year career as a journalist. As soon as she figured out that making up the facts was a whole lot more fun than reporting them, she turned to fiction and never looked back.

Ninie now writes suspense--every flavor except pistachio: psychological suspense, inspirational suspense, suspense thrillers, paranormal suspense, suspense mysteries.

In every book she keeps this promise to her Loyal Reader: "I will tell you a story in a distinctive voice you'll always recognize, about people as ordinary as you are--people who have been slammed by something they didn't sign on for, and now they must fight for their lives. Then smack in the middle of their everyday worlds, those people encounter the unexplainable--and it's always the game-changer."

Also By Ninie Hammon

Nowhere, USA

The Jabberwock

Mad Dog

Trapped

The Hanging Judge

The Witch of Gideon

Blown Away

Nowhere People

The Taken Saga

The Taken

The Changed

The Hidden

The Saved

Through The Canvas Series

Black Water

Red Web

Gold Promise

Blue Tears

The Unexplainable Collection

Five Days in May

Black Sunshine

The Based on True Stories Collection

Home Grown

Sudan

When Butterflies Cry

The Knowing Series

The Knowing

The Deceiving

The Reckoning

The Fault

Stand-alone Psychological Thrillers

The Memory Closet

The Last Safe Place